F,

Also available in Large Print
by Grace Livingston Hill:

Amorelle
Blue Ruin
The Enchanted Barn

EP

FOUND TREASURE

Grace Livingston Hill

T

G.K.HALL&CO.
Boston, Massachusetts
1990

Published in Large Print by arrangement with
Harper and Row Publishers, Inc.

G.K. Hall Large Print Book Series.

Set in 16 pt. Plantin.

Library of Congress Cataloging in Publication Data

Hill, Grace Livingston, 1865-1947.
    Found treasure / by Grace Livingston Hill.
        p.   cm.—(G.K. Hall large print book series) (Nightingale
    series)
        ISBN 0-8161-4930-5 (lg. print)
        1. Large type books.   I. Title.
    [PS3515.I486F68   1990]
    813'.52—dc20   89-27115

"A good name is rather to be chosen than great riches, and loving favor than silver and gold."

Proverbs 22:1.

FOUND TREASURE

Chapter One

THE younger set were meeting in Ethel Garner's summerhouse to make plans for an automobile ride and an all-day picnic which was arranged for the next week.

They fluttered in by ones and twos in their little bright dresses looking like a lot of dressy dolls on the Garner lawn. They hovered about awaiting a few more arrivals, chattering like a flock of birds just alighted.

"O Ethel!" screamed her special chum Janet Chipley, "isn't that a darling new dress! Did your mother make it or did you get it in the city?"

"This?" said Ethel with a conscious look at the dainty little blue-and-white voile she was wearing. "Oh, it's a little imported frock Mother picked up. It is rather good, isn't it?"

"Imported!" exclaimed Maud Bradley

dashing into the conversation with a gusto. "My goodness! They don't import *cotton* dresses do they? Aren't you some swell wearing imported dresses in the afternoon. Say, Ethel, you look precious in it, though, don't you? That's a pastel shade of blue isn't it? You ought to save it for the ride. It's awfully becoming. Jessie Heath said she was getting a new dress, too, her mother ordered it in New York from that great dressmaker she goes to every spring. It's some new kind of pink they're wearing in Paris. But I'm sure it won't be any prettier than yours."

"You've got a pretty dress, too, Maud," said Ethel somewhat patronizingly. "Did you make it yourself?"

"Yes," said Maud with a grimace, "sat up till after midnight last night to finish the hemstitching."

"Aren't you clever! You don't mean to say you did all that hemstitching? Why it looks just like the imported things. I think you are simply great to be able to do it!"

"Oh, that's nothing," said Maud, "I'd much rather do it than study Latin. You know I flunked the exam this year. I get more and more disgusted with it. Say, girls, what do you think? I heard Miss House

2

wasn't going to teach Latin next year. Wouldn't that be great? I'd almost be willing to go back to school another year just to be rid of her. My, she was a pain! How anybody could get like that puzzles me! But isn't it great that we're done high school? You couldn't drag me to college. Emily Morehouse says she's going, and Reitha Kent. But they always were grinds."

"Well, I'm going," said Ethel with satisfaction.

"*You're* going!" screamed her friends in dismay. "Why, I thought you said you weren't."

"Well, so I did, but Mother has persuaded me. She says she wants me to get the *atmosphere!* And you really aren't *anywhere* if you haven't been to college these days!"

"Mercy!" said Janet. "Then I suppose I'll have to go too! I only begged off by telling Dad and Mother you aren't going."

"Oh, come on, Jan, of course you'll go! I couldn't leave you behind. And besides we'll have heaps of fun."

"But we aren't signed up anywhere."

"Yes we are, that is I am, and I know Dad can get you in at my college. He's something on the board. Get your father and mother to come over to-night and talk it over with Dad. He'll fix it. There comes Gladys Harper. Come on girls, let's go back to the summerhouse. The rest will know where to find us, and it's too hot to stay here in the sun. Was that the phone, Flora?" called Ethel as her younger sister came out on the piazza. "Who called? I hope nobody is staying away."

"It was Eleanor Martin. She can't come till half past four. They've got the dress-maker there and she has to be fitted."

"I know," said Ethel, "Come on we're going around to the summerhouse. I wonder what she had to telephone for? She told me that this morning."

Flora in her bright pink organdy followed the girls around to the summerhouse.

"Why, it was about Effie," she admitted with a troubled look as they drifted into the big rustic arbor against its background of tall privet hedge, and settled down among the cushions with which it was amply furnished.

"You know Effie Martin wants to go with us on the picnic. Eleanor is taking their big new car, and Effie wants to drive it part of the time. She asked me to get her an invitation. But Eleanor has found it out, and she doesn't want her to go."

"The very idea!" said Janet Chipley sharply. "Why that would be ridiculous! Why, *she* doesn't belong to our crowd at all!"

"Well, she evidently wants to," said Flora with a troubled sigh, "and I promised her I'd do my best to get her an invitation. She's simply wild to go. And it's really the first time she's ever seemed to care much. What could I do but promise?"

"Well, she's not going to get any invitation if *I'm* on the committee," announced Maud Bradley. "I'll tell you that! Why, she's *unbearable*. Nobody else would want to go if she went, that's certain! Just tell her we had our list all made up and there wasn't room, Flora!"

"But she'd say she could ride on the running board," said Flora, still troubled. Flora did not like to be unkind.

"Yes, that's just what she would do!" asserted Ethel. "Anything to make a sensation! And she doesn't seem to know how disgusting she is. She has a disagreeable habit for every minute in the day, I believe. She bites her nails continually. It sends shivers down my back. I sat behind her in

5

church last Sunday and I nearly went wild! She just took each finger in turn and chewed right around them, and then she put one knee over the other and swung her foot, jarring her knee against the pew in front where that meek little Mrs. Elder sits. I thought I should shriek, she made me so nervous. Mrs. Elder kept turning her head just a little and looking distressed, but she couldn't get the courage to turn clear around and look her in the face and make her stop. I almost disgraced myself sighing with nervousness. I'm sure she heard me, but it didn't make any difference. She didn't even know what it was all about. She turned and stared at me a minute with those great, black eyes of her and kept right on. I don't want any worse punishment than to be obliged to sit beside her in any gathering again."

"Yes, I know just how she is," chimed in Maud Bradley. "She just fidgets and fidgets. She's for all the world as bad as her eight-year-old brother, and he is the most disagreeable little kid in the whole town. *I* sat beside her in church one Sunday when our seat was full, and I was glad when the service was over. She kept turning and twisting and fixing her hat and smoothing her gloves. She had gloves on, so she couldn't bite her nails then. She hummed the tunes while the minister was reading the hymns, and she tore a paper into small bits while the prayer was going on. I didn't have a minute's peace. I'm sure I don't know how anybody could be expected to enjoy her company. She's enough to spoil things wherever she goes. By all means, don't let us invite her. Don't you say so Cornelia? Wouldn't it simply spoil everything if Effie Martin went along with us?"

Cornelia Gilson, a flashy little girl with copper-colored bobbed hair and a yellow frock, had come in while they were talking and listened with an indignant frown.

"What! That Martin girl? Eleanor's kid sister? Well, I should say so!" she answered quickly. "What are you all thinking about? Why should *she* be invited? She never was before!"

Janet Chipley essayed to explain.

"Why Flora Garner says she told her she wanted to go just awfully, and now they have the new car, and Eleanor is to be allowed to take it, and she thinks the girls will ask her."

"Well, we certainly will not!" declared Cornelia indignantly. "She'll find she is mistaken. I should think her own sister would make her understand that. She is not old enough for our crowd. She's only fourteen."

"Well, I guess she's fifteen," reluctantly admitted Maud; "but she doesn't act like it."

"Girls, you're all mistaken about her age; she's sixteen. Her birthday was last week," spoke up Flora Garner timidly. "She wants to go dreadfully. Her sister doesn't want her to one bit, and she didn't want to ask her to secure an invitation, so she asked me. I felt awfully embarrassed, for I didn't know what to say."

"Sixteen! Well, I should think she would be ashamed! Why, she acts like a big tough boy. Last summer at the shore she came tearing down the boardwalk with her hair flying, chasing Tom Moore, and bound to catch him before they reached the bath-houses. I felt awfully humiliated to have her come up to me a few minutes after, when I was talking to Mrs. Earle and her son, and say, 'Hello, Jan!' She was chewing gum, too; and think of it, I had to introduce her! Mrs. Earle is so sweet, she takes in everybody, and she put out her hand and said, 'Is this your cousin, Janet?' Then, after, I told who she was, Mrs. Earle drew her aside and

8

told her softly, so that her son would not hear, and with a great many 'my dears,' that there was a big tear in her skirt; and what do you think that poor fish did? She just laughed out loud and pulled the tear around and stuck her finger in it and said, so that Lawrence Earle couldn't help hearing, 'Oh, yes, I know it. That's been there two weeks. Most everybody's told me of it now. It's too much trouble to mend it down here. It's bad enough to have to sew when I'm at home.' Just then Tom Moore came in sight again, and without saying good-bye or anything, she started and ran, calling, 'Ho, Tom, you can't catch me again! I dare you to!' I was so mortified I could have sunk down into the sand with a good will and never come up again. Lawrence Earle looked after her with the most curious expression. If she could have seen him she would never have held up her head again."

"Oh, yes, she would, Janet," said Maud laughingly. "You don't suppose a little thing like that would bother her! Why, she's got brass enough to make a pair of candlesticks. The thing I don't understand is how she happened to be so utterly ill-mannered, with so lovely a mother."

"Well, surely, girls," said Ethel Garner,

9

"if her own sister doesn't want her, we can't ask her to go along. What is the use of discussing her any further? I, for one, am tired of the subject. She is full of disagreeableness, and apparently has not a single virtue."

"You're forgetting, Ethel," put in Janet Chipley sarcastically, "she can ride a bicycle!"

"Oh, yes, she can ride a wheel," laughed Ethel with a sneer and a curl of her lip, "but she does even that like a clown. She would rather stand on the saddle with one toe and go flying down Main Street than anything else in the world. She just wants to show off her acrobatic feats! I can't understand why her mother lets her. She's too old to ride a bicycle. None of the other girls do."

"You were just saying she wasn't old enough to go with us," urged Flora mischievously.

"Well, you know perfectly what I mean, Flo. Don't try to be clever! She acts just like a great big overgrown small boy. And the way she plays baseball, and tries to get in with the boys! She thinks she's so smart because they praise the way she pitches. She thinks it's so wonderful to be able to pitch like a boy! I think it's unladylike. And she goes whistling through the streets, and she never looks even *neat!* Her clothes are simply a mess! And her hair is a fright! If she went along she'd be sure to disgrace us all in some way. Decidedly, no! She's a flat tire if there ever was one. Don't you all say so, girls?"

"Yes I do," said Maud Bradley. "Come, let's drop her and get to work. There's the route, and the time, and the lunch to plan for, and the afternoon is going fast."

The little company of gaily-dressed girls, settled themselves in the hammocks and chairs that were plentiful in the summer-house and went to work in earnest.

Meantime, on the other side of the carefully trimmed hedge, stretched full length on the soft springy, sweet-smelling earth, her elbows on a mossy bank, her face in her hands, her cheeks very red, her eyes on an open book, lay Effie Martin, the subject of all this conversation. She had taken her book after dinner and slipped off to this group of trees between her father's lawn and that of Mr. Garner's. It was a favorite retreat for her, away from the noise of her teasing brother, and the possible calls of conscience, when she heard the work of the house going

11

on, and knew that she ought to be helping. She did not like to work, and she did love to read. She often came here when she wanted to be alone. She had found this particular bit of mossy turf, covered by clean spicy, pine needles. She did not know that in the summer arbor, opposite, Ethel and Flora Garner would receive their friends that day.

She would not have hesitated on that account if she had known. It did not occur to her that she would be liable to hear conversations not meant for her ears. When she had first heard voices approaching the hedge on the other side, she had paid little heed to them, but had read on until she suddenly heard her own name and became aware that she was the subject of much unpleasant remark. Her cheeks flamed with anger, and her big, black eyes sparkled dangerously. It did not occur to her that she was an eavesdropper, or that she ought to get up and go away. She would probably not have gone if it had occurred to her. It had never been very fully impressed upon her that there was anything wrong in listening to what is not intended for one's ears, especially when the theme is one's self.

The girls on the other side of the hedge

12

went on discussing her personal habits. It had never occurred to her that she had personal habits before, or that those habits could be agreeable or disagreeable to others. There was something startling in hearing them portrayed in such unpleasant tones. Her heart beat fast with indignation. So this was what they thought of her. Her first impulse was to start to her feet and rush into their midst; but what could she do? They were but stating their opinions.

She had half started to get up, but now she sank back again. Alas! she could not deny the statements they had made about her, either. She glanced down at her stubby fingers whose nails, worn to the quick, gave sad evidence of being daily bitten. Now that she recalled it, she supposed she did bite her nails in church. She was tired and longed to get out of doors, and that seemed to give her relief from what seemed to her a dull meeting. She glanced down at her dress. It was even now torn and spotted in many places. She had never paid much attention to her clothes before. She had not minded a few spot or rents, more or less. Now she suddenly saw what others thought of her. How they went on scoring her—those girls of whose circle she had so earnestly aspired to be one! How she hated them for it! What a hateful world she was in! How could they talk that way? Those pretty, simpering girls who could not ride as she could—not one of them, nor pitch a ball so that the boys would as soon have her in the game as one of themselves! They had nothing but non-sense in their heads, and were very silly. Why should she care what they said? But all the time, as the talk went on, her cheeks burned redder and redder and her heart throbbed with its painful mingling of emo-tions.

Meanwhile the girls, unaware of the an-gry little listener on the other side of the hedge, arranged their program. They were to rest and refresh themselves at a farm-house, a pleasant distance from home, and return in the evening by moonlight, if the the night was clear. Then came the question of the chosen guests. All the usual girls were named, Eleanor Martin, Effie's older sister, among the rest. A spasm of almost hatred again passed over Effie, as she thought of the selfishness of her sister, who was unwill-ing that she should take part in the coming pleasure. Eleanor could have managed it for her if she had chosen, but Eleanor was nine-teen, and did not care to be troubled by "kids," as she chose to designate her sister, albeit she never breathed this in the presence of their mother. Mrs. Martin disliked slang, and endeavored, as much as in her lay, to bring up her daughters properly; but it was a hard task with so many feet to guide, so many mouths to feed, so little in the family treasury. This was, perhaps, the reason that poor Effie had been so often obliged to shift for herself.

The letters in the book before her were all blurred into one long word. Effie felt no further interest in the hero of the historical novel that she had been reading. History was empty and void. Her own life had loomed up and eclipsed the ages; so that there was nothing of interest outside it. She felt that no one had ever been so miserable, so helpless, so disliked, so ill-treated, so utterly unhappy as herself. How could she go on living after to-day? She had suddenly seen herself as others saw her. Her feelings must have had a little touch of what Eve felt when she had eaten of that forbidden fruit and no longer saw the world about her fair. How could she ever endure it? Her thoughts surged through her brain without beginning or end; and through it all she longed to jump through that hedge, with vengeance in her eyes, and pounce upon those hateful girls and make them take it all back; make them suffer for what they had said, or do something that should assuage this dreadful feeling that oppressed her.

The planning on the other side of the hedge went on. The anticipated pleasure was discussed with animation. This was heightened somewhat by the arrival of a little sister of Janet Chipley, who brought a book her sister had sent her after, and contributed this information as she was running away again to play: "Say, Janet, did you know Lawrence Earle had come home? I saw him just now coming from the station in the car with his mother, and he's going to be home all summer, for he said so, and he's going to play tennis with me a lot, for he's promised. Isn't that lovely? And he isn't a bit different from a year ago, if he *has* been to college. I thought perhaps you'd like to ask him to your ride," and Bessie Chipley flew away to her game, leaving the girls in high glee over the arrival of the young man, who had won a most brilliant record in a noted college, and for whose society the girls were all eager.

"Oh, isn't that lovely!" "Of course we'll ask him!" were some of the exclamations from the delighted girls. But the listener, on the other side of the hedge, only felt the blood burn hotter in her cheeks as she remembered what the girls had said she had done the year before at the seashore; and that this young man had been a witness. She really felt humiliation on her own account now, as she realized how she must have appeared in his eyes, tearing along like a boy, and careless about the great rent in her gown. A year ago she would scarcely have understood why this should have been embarrassing, so much of a child had she been; but now young womanhood was stirring in her heart, with a sense of pride, self-consciousness, and the fitness of things. Self-consciousness, had been very slight indeed, until now, but her eyes had been opened and she was ashamed and Lawrence Earle of all people! The boy who had taught her to pitch a ball when she was a mere infant. Of course, he was a great deal older than she was—five or six years at least, and had probably forgotten all about her. But she had always remembered him as an ideal hero!

"We must have another girl to make even couples," they were saying, and Effie's humiliation was so complete that she scarcely felt the pang of disappointment that she could not be chosen for that vacant place. No; rather stay at home for ever, than that she should be of the same company with that immaculate youth who had witnessed her degradation. This was what she felt. Suddenly her feelings rose to such a pitch she could no longer keep still, and, scrambling to her feet, she fairly fled from the place where she had so suffered. The tears had gathered in her eyes, and once she fell with a stinging thud to the ground, having tripped over a hidden root. This only brought the tears the faster, and when she reached the house she threw her book upon the floor, ran through the house, slamming all the doors after her, tore up the stairs to her own room, where she locked herself in, and threw herself upon the bed in an agony of weeping such as she had very seldom experienced.

And her patient mother, who had been trying to take a nap with the fretful, teething baby, was awakened by her rushing through the house and sighed, "Oh, there goes Effie. What shall we do with that child?"

Chapter Two

EFFIE had cried perhaps half an hour. Hers was too vehement a nature to do things by halves, and her weeping was so violent that she was thoroughly exhausted. Then she lay still and began to think things over. Why was it that those girls disliked her, and that she seemed to be so unwelcome everywhere? For now that she thought of it, she saw that there were quite a number of people in the world who did not care to have her around. Her mother loved her, she felt sure, but somehow her mother always sighed when she came into the room. Why was that? Was she not wanted in the world? She could not help it, she supposed, or, could she? What the girls had said about some things was quite true, though she had never felt before that they were things that mattered to others. If she wanted to bite her finger nails, what business was it of theirs? She never troubled their finger nails. She had a right to do with her own as she pleased, so long as she let other people's alone. But here it seemed that these personal habits of hers did trouble other people, and she must not expect to be wanted if she could not make herself pleasant. She looked at her stumpy fingers through her tear-dimmed eyes. They certainly did not look pretty. But it had never occurred to her that biting them had anything to do with that.

The girls had said that she made them nervous. She hardly understood why, but if it was so, why, of course, it was. The question was, could she stop doing it? And if she could, and should, would that make any difference in the feeling of those girls for her? But then, she did not intend to try to please those girls! No, indeed! They were not worth pleasing. But there were people in the world to whom she would like to seem lovely—her mother, for instance, and perhaps Flora Garner, for she had been nice and sweet about asking to have her invited to the ride. Everybody said Flora Garner was sweet. She had that reputation wherever she was known. It was a great thing to have people feel that way about you and say

20

nice things. And then her poor swollen cheeks burned again at thought of the hateful things that had been said about her. But would it be worth while to try to make things better so that people might think well of her? A fierce desire to get on her wheel and fly away, into the gathering shades of the dusky night that was drawing on, seized her. It was supper time, but she wanted no supper. She would go, and she jerked herself up from the bed, caught her hat, and without waiting to wash the tear stains from her face, dashed downstairs. It was like her. Effie always did everything without thinking. As she went out of the door she heard her mother sigh and say to her baby brother: "Oh, baby, baby, if you would only just sit still on the floor for ten minutes longer till I finish this seam. My back aches so that I cannot hold you and sew any longer."

Effie went straight on out of the door, feeling sorry for her mother, having a dim sense that the baby was unreasonable, and life hard, anyway; but it never occurred to her that she had anything to do with it until she was flying along the smooth road fully a mile from home, and the fresh breeze fanning her face had somewhat cooled the tempest in her heart. She was beginning to feel more like herself, and trying to decide if there was any way in which she might change that would affect the feelings of others toward her. There was Mother, for instance, again—yes, Mother, sitting in the gathering shadows at this moment, stealing the last rays of light, to sew the dark garment that she expected to wear on the morrow, to pay her last tribute to a dear old school friend who was done with his life. Mother's little excursions and holidays, somehow, were almost always set apart for last sad rites and duties of neighborly kindness. It was strange about Mother, how she never seemed to have any good times for her own. Effie never thought of it before. How nice it would be if Mother was on a wheel, flying along by her side! But Mother on a wheel! How funny it would be! She couldn't learn to ride in the first place, she was so timid. And then how could she get time? She was at this minute doing two things at once, and that baby was very hard to take care of. It was hard that Mother couldn't even get her dress done without being hindered! Well! There was something! Why had she not thought of that before?

She turned her wheel so suddenly that a little dog who was trotting along in the road, thinking he knew just where she was going, almost got his tail cut off.

Back she flew faster than she had come, and bursting in at the door threw her hat on a chair, and grabbed the baby from the floor at his mother's feet where he was vainly endeavoring to pull himself up to a standing posture by her skirt. Mrs. Martin gave a nervous jump as Effie entered, and another with an anxious "Oh, take care, Effie!" as the baby was tossed into the air. But Effie, intent on doing good for once in her life, was doing it as she did everything else, with a vengeance, and she went on tossing the baby higher and higher, regardless of her mother's protests. Each crow of the baby made Effie more eager to amuse him. She whirled around the room with him in her arms, tumbling over a chair occasionally, but not minding that in the least, she danced along to the middle of the room under the gas fixture, and just as her mother rose hastily, and dropped her sewing, saying, "Effie, I insist——" she tossed the excited baby high into the air, and brought the curly head sharp against the chandelier. Then the fun ceased. The baby screamed, and the mother rushed and caught him to her breast, and with reproachful looks at the penitent Effie, sent for hot water and Pond's Extract. The others coming in gathered around the darling of the house, and hesitated not to reproach Effie for her part in the mischief until her anger flamed forth, and seeing that the baby had recovered, and was apparently not seriously injured, she rushed from the room to her own in another torrent of weeping. Ths time she knelt before the open window and watched the lights through her tears as they peeped out here and there over the village, and felt bitter toward them and toward everything. Why should she be the one always to blame for everything that happened? Here she had given up her ride when she was having a good time, and had come home to help Mother and was greeted only with an exclamation of fear, and then this had happened—a thing that might have happened if he had been with any of the others, she thought; she was scolded for what she had intended should be a relief and a help to Mother, and that was all the good she had done. Much progress she had made in her own reformation! She would not be likely to go on in it very far if this was the result of her first trial, and her heart grew hard and bitter again.

By and by the dinner bell rang and she went sulkily down and took her place and ate in silence, until Eleanor, full of her afternoon, put another sting in the already very sore heart of her sister. It appeared that she had gone to the committee meeting at Garner's, probably after her sister had left the hedge.

"Mamma," she said with the haughtiness of her lately acquired young ladyhood, "I do wish you would reprove Effie. She is forever making herself obnoxious. I found out that she has been poking around trying to get in with our crowd. She's nothing but a child!"

"It's an awful pity you and Eff have to live in the same town with each other, Nell, she gives you so much trouble," put in Johnnie, the outspoken younger brother.

"Johnnie, you're very saucy, and that isn't smart at all," responded Eleanor, flattening her eyelids down in a way she had that she fancied was very reproving to her brother.

"Mamma, I wish you would tell Effie that you won't allow her under any circumstances to go with us next week on our ride. She is getting very troublesome. I——"

But Eleanor was interrupted by Effie, whose black eyes flashed fire and tears as she rose from the table, her dinner only half finished.

"It isn't in the least necessary for you to ask Mamma to do any such thing. I wouldn't go if you dragged me! I know exactly every word those precious girls of yours have said about me this afternoon, and they are a mean, selfish lot, who care nothing about anything but clothes! I only hope you'll enjoy the company of those who speak that way about your sister. I should not, not even if they had been talking about *you*. But you may rest easy about me, I shall not trouble you any more. I've been made to understand most thoroughly that nobody in this world wants me. I am sure I can't tell what I was made for, anyway," and with a voice that trembled with her utter humiliation and defeat she stalked from the room, her lifted chin and haughty manner barely lasting till the dining-room door shut her from the family gaze, when she burst into uncontrolled tears and rushed upstairs for the third time that day to her own little room.

"Why, what does this mean, Eleanor?" asked the pained voice of the father, laying down the evening paper behind which he had been somewhat shielded from the avalanche of talk about him. "What have you done to the child? Why hasn't she as much right to go riding as the rest of you? I thought that was why we bought the seven-passenger car, so there would be plenty of room for anybody that wanted to go?"

"You don't understand," said Eleanor with reddening cheeks, and she essayed to explain to her father the fine distinction of age and class in the society in which she moved, but somehow her father could not be made to understand, and the end of it was that Eleanor was told that if her sister was not welcomed on the ride, then she could not go. Rebellious and angrier than ever at Effie, she declared she would stay at home then. So it came about that the Martin household was not in a happy frame of mind that evening at the close of their evening meal. And the two sisters lay down to rest with hard thoughts of each other.

Effie, as she turned her light out, knelt a moment beside her window to look at the stars, and murmur the form of prayer that had been so much a part of her bringing up that she scarcely realized what it all meant. "Help me to be good," was one of the oft-repeated sentences, and Effie no longer felt it necessary for her thoughts to stay by

27

to see that these words were spoken to the One above who was supposed to be her guard and guide. She fancied herself on the whole rather good as goodness in girls went. Now, to-night, as she finished her petition, which was rather a repetition, she looked up to the stars she loved, and thought of a scrap of poetry she had picked up in her reading, which she was not well enough taught to know was wonderful. It ran thus:

All that I know
  Of a certain star
Is, it can throw
  (Like the angled spar)
Now a dart of red,
Now a dart of blue;
Till my friends have said
  They would fain see too,
My star that dartles the red and the blue!
Then it stops like a bird; like a flower
    hangs furled:
  They must solace themselves with the
    Saturn above it
What matter to me if their star is a world?
  Mine has opened its soul to me; therefore
    I love it.

Poor little, lonely, disagreeable Effie

wished as she looked out into the night that she could be like a star, and be able to dartle red and blue for some one, so that others might hear of it and want to see her and know her. How nice that would be! That star language evidently meant people, and it meant there was some one somewhere who could see beauties in some star everybody could not see. She wondered if ever anybody would think they saw any thing good like dartles of red and blue in her, and would feel that they didn't care after that whether other people's worlds were great or not so long as they had her red and blue dartles.

But how silly such thoughts were! If those hateful girls who had talked about her that afternoon had known she had thoughts like this how they would have screeched with laughter! Her cheeks burned hotly in the darkness at the very thought and she arose and slammed the window down, warm night though it was, and went to bed feeling utterly miserable. How was it possible for her ever to be different? She could not. She had tried that afternoon, and failed most miserably, and she was not one who was likely to try again in the same direction.

Was there anywhere else to turn? Oh, if

she but had some wise and good helper who would tell what was the matter, and if she must go on being hated all her life as she had begun.

Then the thought of what the girls had said about her clothes came and drowned all other thoughts, and she drifted off to sleep planning how she would fix up an old dress that should be the envy of all the town.

Poor child, she was only a little girl yet at heart, and was just waking up to the fact that she was growing up and a great deal more would be expected of her.

Perchance her guardian angel standing by, remembering that she was dear to her Heavenly Father, and knowing for a surety that there was light coming to her darkened pathway, brushed the tears in pity from her young face, for she dreamed that a soft hand touched her forehead and cooled and comforted her.

But downstairs Effie's father and mother were having a serious conference about her.

"I'm sure I don't know what to do with her," her anxious mother was saying. "She grows more heartless and careless every day. To-day she nearly killed the baby with her impetuosity, and when I tried to stop her before she hit his head against the chandelier she simply ignored my commands. I wonder if it would do any good to send her away to school. I never believed much in finishing schools, but Effie really needs something to tone her down. She goes rushing through life without any idea of manners or any thought of others. I'm sure I don't see how we came to have a child like that!"

"I am afraid nobody understands her," said her father with troubled brows. "She seems to me so much like my own little sister Euphemia for whom she is named, and she was a wild little loving thing like Effie, but she would fly up into flinders if people were unjust to her—"

"Nobody has been unjust to Effie," said her mother coldly. "Everybody would love her if she would be less selfish and rude. I have tried to tell her but she doesn't even seem to hear me. And Sam, she isn't in the least like your sister Euphemia. She was mild and gentle and lovely as I remember her. We should have named Effie Joan of Arc or some outlandish masculine name, for she never will be anything but a disgrace to your sister's name, I'm afraid."

"Oh, don't say that Hester," said the father in a pained voice. "I'm sure our little

31

Euphemia will grow up some day and understand. If you would just try to talk with her a little about it——"

"Talk with her!" said her mother wearily. "I've talked and talked and it rolls right off from her. She goes tearing in one door and out the other on her own affairs, and never minds whether I have a headache or whether the baby is asleep, or whether there are dishes to be washed on the maid's day out! She seems a hopeless case!"

"Now, now, Mother. You mustn't talk that way about our little girl. I sometimes think perhaps the other children put upon her. Eleanor now is a bit overbearing since she has grown up, and she wants to have the whole right to the car. That really isn't just to Euphemia. The child has as good a right to go on that ride as she."

"Not if the other girls don't want her," said the mother. "They feel themselves older you know——"

"But they're not much older are they? Eleanor is only two years older than Euphemia. That ought not to be such a great difference. And those Garner girls, why the youngest one was born two days later than Euphemia, for I remember congratulating her father on her birth. There is something wrong somewhere. Why don't they want Euphemia? Aren't her clothes right?"

"Why, yes—" said her mother hesitantly, a new trouble gathering in her eyes. "She is as well dressed for her age as need be. She has never complained. She doesn't care much for dress. She always preferred getting out and away to play ball or hockey or skate, no matter what she had on."

"Well, perhaps that's it," said the pitying father. "Perhaps she needs something a little more fancy, Mother. We haven't realized that she was growing up too, and needed things. She ought to be dressed right of course. I know you've been trying to economize so we could get the car, but things are beginning to look up at the office a little, and I think pretty soon we'll have things a little easier. You get Euphemia what she wants, Mother. I can't bear to have her look the way she did to-night. It isn't right for a child."

"But she really has never expressed a desire for new clothes," said her mother thoughtfully. "All she wants is to get off on that wheel of hers. I'm afraid she'll never grow up."

"There are worse faults than that, Mother,

worse faults. I believe it might be worse to grow up too soon."

"Yes," sighed the mother, "I'm afraid Eleanor has done that. She seems really hard on her sister sometimes, although I think it's just because she's so sensitive about what the other girls think. Eleanor is a good girl."

"Well she is all wrong in this matter. She really has no right to cut her sister out of going on a ride."

"Now Father, I'm not so sure," said the mother. "You know Eleanor didn't get it up. The girls invited her, and they didn't ask Effie."

"Well they should have! They asked for the car, didn't they?"

"Well, but that didn't make it necessary for them to ask all of the children, and Effie has never been in that crowd."

"Well, if she wants to go now I think she has a right!" declared the father.

"No, not unless she has made herself welcome. I'm afraid it is Effie's own fault that she is not invited."

"Well, Mother, you look into the matter and see if there can't be something done for Euphemia. I can't have my sister's name-sake turning out a failure in life, and that's what she'll be if something isn't done for her. I'm afraid I shall never forget her face when she said she didn't know what she was born for anyway, and that she had found out there wasn't any place in the world where she was wanted. That's a pretty serious thing for a girl to get into her head, I think!"

"It isn't likely that she really meant all that," said her mother. "She was just angry. She'll likely have forgotten it all by to-morrow. I never heard her say anything like that before. She usually doesn't care in the least what people think about her. She is utterly independent and goes her own way, no matter what anybody says. She is more like a boy than a girl."

"I can't think that, Mother," said Effie's father shaking his head. "There was a real depth to her tones. You look into it and see if you can't get at the inwardness of this thing. Somebody must have done something pretty ugly to her to make her look as she did at the dinner table to-night."

But the next morning Effie came swinging downstairs whistling in loud piercing tones and waking the baby who had had a bad night with two teeth he was cutting and had just dropped off to sleep. Both father and mother looked at her with stern eyes and sharp reproofs. Indeed, to the newly

35

awakened Effie their words were so unjust and cutting that she slammed out of the back door without her breakfast and jumping on her bicycle rode off into the country and spent a furious two hours pedalling away and thinking hard thoughts of her parents, her sisters, all the girls in the town, and her world in general, finally working off the surplus fury, and coasting back down the hills toward home another way around, whistling gaily to keep up her courage. No one should know how hard she was hit and how much she cared that no one loved her. Let them all be hateful to her if they would. She could stand it, and she would see if she could not beat them all in spite of everything. Maybe if she got her dress fixed up they would think more of her. Now she thought about it everybody was always loving and nice to Nell when she had a new dress on. Nell could get anything out of her father when she was dressed up. Dress must make a great difference in this world. She had always scorned it as among the necessary bothers of living. Now she began to see that it might be a desirable accessory. At least she would try it.

She rode into the yard with grim determination upon her face, skirted the driveway, and entered by way of the kitchen. She secured a few crackers, an orange, and some cake and stole up the back stairs to her room, where she set herself to examine her wardrobe and see what could be done with it.

Chapter Three

IT was like Effie not to take any one into her confidence, but to embark on her new enterprise alone. She even took some of her own hoarded money which she had been saving to buy a new tennis racket and went and bought some fashion magazines instead of going down and asking Mother for hers. She had a feeling that if she worked this thing out it had to be done wholly on her own initiative. Nobody else must know. In fact she felt if anybody did find out that she was trying to be different she would certainly have to stop trying.

All the spare time that Effie had, outside of the duties actually required of her, she spent in her room, with an occasional intermission when she would mount her bicycle and ride afar furiously, returning to a new attack upon her self-imposed task. She meant to get that new dress done by the day of the ride! Not for any special hope or reason which she entertained, not for the possibility of being seen by any of the party, for she scorned such praise, but just for her own satisfaction, she wanted to get that dress done before the day of the ride.

If any one had been in the habit of noticing Effie's movements she certainly would have excited the family curiosity now, for it was unheard of that she should remain in the house while the great out-of-doors called her. If they thought anything about it or noticed that she did not go out so much, or was absent from the public tennis courts, or the baseball field where she had been wont to hover, they merely thought she was off in the hammock somewhere reading. Nobody paid much heed to Effie from morning to night, except to blame her or complain of her. Only the mother, with her reawakened anxiety, watched her, listened at the hall door for her step, hovered near her locked door, anxious lest some new phase of this ugly duckling's development was in process of being evolved, relieved that no apparent catastrophe seemed to result from her long sessions in her room.

For Effie had decided in the course of her

meditations, that the very first thing needed in the building of a noteworthy character was a neat and stylish sport suit that she could wear on her wheel or for tennis or golf, if she ever got a chance to play. And while that is perhaps not the usual way for a young person to set about living a different life, nevertheless her mother and her guardian angel were pleased.

Effie was not fond of sewing, neither was she an adept in that art, for she loved her books and her outdoor life too dearly; but she was ever one who, if her will and desire were great enough, could do almost anything she tried to. So it was not surprising as the days went by that she really was accomplishing marvels in the way of making quite a pretty sport dress out of her sister's old school dress, having actually thought so far as carefully to rip, clean, and press it before beginning to make it up.

Effie had also surprised her father and sister when she found out what commands her father had laid upon Eleanor concerning the ride. She had gone to him and asked him to allow Eleanor to go, telling him that she honestly did not wish to go, and would not feel at all happy to have Eleanor kept at home. This she did, not because she had attained any great degree of self-sacrifice in her spirit, but being of a practical turn of mind, she saw no sort of use in keeping her sister away from a pleasure which she knew by personal yearnings she would enjoy so much, just because she, Effie, was debarred from it. Furthermore, she knew that Eleanor would be sure to tell the girls why she could not go, and they would probably feel obliged to ask her for Eleanor's sake, and she wanted to have nothing more to do with that ride. Her cheeks burned with the thought of it. Ugly ride! And ugly day when she had lain and listened to a description of herself as others saw her. She felt as if she had grown years older since then. Now and then when pride and pleasure in her new dress would lift her up beyond her gloomy thoughts, there would come to her with a sudden pang the thought: what is the use of making it when I am not wanted anywhere to wear it? But she kept steadily on, and through her mother's help, given unsuspected here, and there, for the mother had more sympathy with her untamed little girl than the child knew, she actually had it in a wearable condition a few days before the day of the picnic.

And now there was a revelation for the

mother, for she found that Effie, her third daughter, the girl who was always a tomboy, and tore her clothes as soon as they were on, or soiled them, or put them on awry, and who had come into the family after so many others that she had been obliged by the force of circumstances, and the state of the family purse, to wear other people's cast-offs so much, now stood arrayed in a dress that fitted her lithe, strong young form, and was neat, trim, and stylish. She was actually pretty. Never had any one called Effie pretty since she was a little baby and the aunt for whom she was named had come to see her and said she was a pretty baby, but it wouldn't last, she could see that with half an eye. Pretty babies always made ugly grown folks, and everybody had repeated that until it came to be a settled fact that Effie was not pretty. She had long ago understood it so herself, and accepted the fact firmly, if a little bitterly. Eleanor, everybody agreed, had beautiful eyes, and with rich complexion and ready wit, was not only handsome, but very bright. But now the mother saw in this other daughter a pretty vision where she had not expected it, and suddenly put her arms around her child's neck, folded her close, and called

41

her "My little Euphemia," as she had called
her when she was a wee baby, and her
mother had had time to sit for three whole
weeks and just love her and cuddle her, and
see all her baby charms.

Effie felt a sudden joy in those words of
her mother's. She was glad that she had
tried to do something, even if it was only to
make a dress. She went back to her room
surveying herself a long time in the glass.
What a difference it made to have a pretty
dress instead of the torn skirt and soiled
blouse she had been wearing. Some hint of
a Bible verse floated through her head—she
was not sure at all that there was such a
verse—something about being clothed upon
with something—righteousness probably.
She wondered if any robe of righteousness
could feel better upon any one than this
little gown she had made with her own
hands.

And then a new idea came to her. Why
not make more dresses?

With Effie to get an idea was to carry it
out, and forthwith she hurried up to the
attic to an old trunk where all the cast-offs
of the family were stowed away.

Fifteen minutes later she came down with
her arms full of faded, soiled georgette.

42

To any one with less determination than Effie the bundle would have looked utterly hopeless. The color had originally been pink, but had faded to a sickly yellowish saffron. But Effie while she ripped off yards of crystal beading, was planning how she would buy a ten-cent package of rose dye and make that discouraged-looking material seem like a summer sunset cloud.

Patiently she ripped and snipped away until at last it was all apart, a seemingly worthless pile of dirty pink. There was one consolation, there was enough of it. For the dress had been made long ago when dresses were long and wide and full of ruffles and shirring and pleats, and there was material enough to make three dresses of the modern kind, if it had all been in good condition.

When it was all apart Effie made a suds of soap flakes and put it asoak while she jumped on her wheel and rode down to the drug store for a package of pink dyeing soap.

An hour later she stood surveying her finished work with satisfaction. The georgette was washed clean, and dyed a lovely shell pink, and lay in soft billows of cloud like a sunset sky on every chair in her room, smooth and apparently as good as new. The last length was stretched smoothly on her bed and pinned firmly inch by inch along the edges. She had discovered that it took each strip from five to ten minutes to become perfectly dry and smooth, and she was overjoyed with the result. Now, she would have a real evening dress. She had always wanted one when Eleanor and the other girls came trooping in with their pretty bright fluffy frocks. Of course, she had no place to wear one but then it would be a joy just to have such a dress hanging in her closet, to know it was there if any occasion ever should come to wear it. She had openly scorned "dolling up" as she called it, but in her secret heart had wished often that she too might look pretty and be admired like the other girls. Well, probably nobody would ever see her in this dress but she meant to have it ready. Perhaps sometime she would put it on and surprise them all and let them see that tomboy Effie could look nice too. Anyhow it would be lots of fun to make it and not let a soul, even Mother, know until it was done. Perhaps if it looked nice Mother would call her little Euphemia. "My little Euphemia." How that warmed her wild young heart! And Mother's tone had been

44

so dear when she had said it! Perhaps she could make her say it again!

She studied the fashion books for a long time to select the right style for this dress, for Effie had ideas even if she had never paid much attention to dress. She wanted it to be prettier than any pink dress she had ever seen before.

She hesitated for a long time as to whether she would finish the edge with picot or with binding, but finally decided on binding. In the first place, there was so much of the material there would be plenty for binding, and while picot would be much easier for her, saving more than half the labor, still it would cost something, and she had already spent more than half of her little hoard. She experimented with a few small pieces of the georgette and found that after some awkwardness she was going to be able to manage the binding, and it somehow appealed to her because it was so exceedingly neat. Picot edges were apt to grow taggy. Eleanor's did. And she wanted nothing about her to suggest untidiness. Those girls should see that she could be as neat and trim as any of them when she tried. She even planned to make a flower for her shoulder out of the pieces of georgette, like the picture in the

45

fashion magazine, and she grew so interested in trying to cut the long slim petals and make them curl up at the edges by drawing them under a pencil-end quickly, that she forgot to go downstairs and set the table for her mother, a duty that was supposed to be hers on the maid's day out. "Heedless Effie!" the family called her, and her cheeks grew red with the truth of the adjective as she hurriedly put aside her materials and rushed downstairs when the dinner bell rang.

She was quite silent at the table, glowering with drawn brows when Eleanor said sarcastic things about how she slipped out of all her duties.

"I suppose you were off with the boys playing ball or something," said Eleanor with a sneer. "I declare, Mamma, I should think you'd be ashamed of having her act like a tough boy! She's getting so big and bony, and she doesn't care how she looks. The other day I was passing the boys' ball field late in the afternoon and here was Effie in that old gray skirt with John's red sweater on and her hair all over her eyes, and she had a baseball bat in her hand and was hitting and running with great strides, kicking up her heels like a wild child. I was mortified to death to think I had a sister like that. I thought when vacation came she would stop playing baseball, but it seems she plays every day——"

"That's a lie!" said Effie rising with fury in her face. "I haven't been out this week! Mother knows I haven't!" and with a glance of reproach at her mother she dashed from the room and rushed to her refuge upstairs. She was so blinded with her tears that she forgot all about that last breadth of georgette pinned out on her bed, and flung herself despairingly right into it, and never knew she had done it until a pin caught her cheek and tore an ugly scratch across its flushed surface.

Downstairs she had left an uncomfortable scene again. Effie's father had risen from the table, white with distress, his lips actually trembling:

"Now, now, children, this must stop!" he said. "I can't have Euphemia treated in this way. Eleanor, you are very much to blame. You have no right to talk that way about your sister before everybody. She is getting almost to hate everybody. You are growing hard and sharp as you grow up. I am distressed beyond measure at your attitude toward your sister."

"Well, do you want me to shut my mouth and let her be made a laughingstock in the town?" retorted Eleanor. "That's what she is. None of the girls will have anything to do with her. She isn't like a girl, she's like a big tough boy. I thought it was my duty to tell you."

"You should come then privately and tell your mother or me. You should not bring Effie out in a disgraceful way before the family. I insist that this must stop. Your sister was generous enough to come and ask that I allow you to take the car and go on your excursion even though your friends were unwilling to invite her, a daughter of the house as much as you are. It seems to me that you reward your sister in a very hateful way."

"Well, you're not around her much, Dad. You don't know how mortifying she is. Why, nobody wants her around. Nobody!"

Eleanor's voice floated up through the open window and came straight to poor Effie's ears and her tears started afresh. How terrible was life when her own sister could say things like that! Oh, if she could only die! If she could only get out of it. Nobody would care, only perhaps her father a little, and well—yes—her mother—remembering

48

her voice when she had said "My little Euphemia!" But after all, if she were gone it would be a relief to everybody. She was only a duty, never a delight. Now see how it had turned out to-day of all days when she had meant to be so good and help her mother! She hadn't done a thing to help. Just stayed in her room and worked for herself. And it would probably always be so. She couldn't be like other girls, and think of things. She couldn't! Oh why should she try! If there was only some one to help her! Some kind friend who would understand, and to whom she was not afraid to go for advice. Perhaps there was a way.

But there wasn't. There was no one in the whole wide world who cared or would help. They expected her to be just what they wanted her to be, and they had no patience with her that she was not, and that was the whole of it! There was no use trying. And why should she bother to make herself pretty clothes? No one would like her any better if she had them. Eleanor would likely laugh and ask her if she was going to play ball in the pink georgette if she did succeed in making it up so it looked like other girls' things.

So she viciously pulled the pins out of the

pretty pink stuff and rolled the whole thing unceremoniously into a box and put it on the top shelf of her closet, resolving never to touch it again. Then she crept into bed and cried herself to sleep.

For what was the use of trying to overcome her name? She had a bad reputation. Everybody expected her to be boisterous and forgetful and rough and uncivil, and they thought she was even when she wasn't. They would say in that superior tone of theirs, "Oh, you can't expect anything else of Euphemia!"

Euphemia! Why did she have to have a hateful name like that? It was a piece of all the rest. She was an odd number with an ugly name. Her hair wouldn't curl and her face was fat, and her bones were large, and she liked to play ball with the boys better than anything else in life, and that was the truth, so what was the use of trying to please anybody anyway?

And at last she fell asleep.

She did not know that a few minutes later her mother coming up with a glass of milk and a plate of nice things found her asleep with the tears on her cheeks, and a sob still in her throat, and that she knelt beside her a long time praying for her dear wild little girl that she might be led into the paths of peace and righteousness, and find out the true secret of right living.

Chapter Four

THE morning of the picnic dawned bright and clear. It seemed as if it had been made especially for the occasion, and Eleanor came down in a pretty new dress which the dressmaker had finished especially for the occasion.

Effie too, donned her new sport dress, but not until after breakfast, and until she had watched her sister leave the house, driving the new car gaily, for the rendezvous at Maud Bradley's.

Then she turned with a long quivering breath of envy and hopelessness, and went to get her little new frock from the closet.

She had not taken it out since the night she hung it there, when her new resolves had suffered such a rebuff. The georgette still reposed in an unceremonious roll in the box on the closet shelf, and she wondered why she had tried anyway to make a sport dress. She couldn't wear it to play ball with the boys very well. She would feel hampered lest she would soil it. She couldn't slide to a base with a pleated silk skirt on, and she couldn't pitch her ball right for fear she would split the shoulders. But anyhow she had decided that she didn't want to play ball with the boys anymore. Eleanor had taken all the pleasure out of that. Eleanor would presently take the joy out of everything she had ever cared to do.

Nevertheless she got herself into the little brown frock, with its simple stylish lines, and its bright touch of burnt orange. It was only Eleanor's old cast-off crêpe de Chine, but it did somehow have an air. It really was quite becoming. It made a soft rose color bloom out in her healthy cheeks, and matched the brown of her eyes and hair. She stared at herself almost in wonder, and somehow her lonely wounded heart felt a little comforted. For it was nice to look pretty and pleasing, almost like other girls!

So she put on her little brown hat, taking unusual care with her thick obstreperous hair to put it into smooth and becoming order, and was amazed again to see what a difference a little care made in her appearance. Well, perhaps it was worth while to look nice anyway, just for her own self, even if no one else noticed it.

She slipped downstairs, taking care that no one saw her as she stole out to the back kitchen where she kept her wheel, and in a moment more was riding off down the street.

It was no part of her plan to come into contact with the excursion party that day. Hateful things! She wouldn't have them see her for the world! It never entered her head that they would not have known her if they had seen her now, riding along in this neat and becoming rig, trim tan shoes and stockings, sitting like a lady on her wheel, her jaws not working rythmically chewing gum, her whole lithe figure poised gracefully. She did not in the least resemble the girl whom they all despised, who usually tore along on her wheel with her head down, shoulders humped, jaws working hard, hair hanging over her eyes untidily, a tear in her skirt, and a hole in the elbow of her brother's old cast-off sweater, and her old canvas sneakers covered with mud. No, they would not have known her.

Her object was to go as far from the planned route of the gay party that day as pleasant roads and her own will could take her, and her mother, watching the trim figure out of sight, so entirely one with the wheel she rode, sighed and wished she might give her a little of the happiness she knew Effie had longed for so much. Then the mother prayed to her Heavenly Father to guide this loved one's footsteps into His ways, and turned back to her baby and her crowding household cares. If she had not been a mother who confided in her Heavenly Father she could not have borne the burdens of her daily life.

Effie's main object was to ride fast and cross the old township road before the party which had planned its route along the highway should reach there. Then she would be far beyond any sight of them, and could forget them, and speed away into the sweet country, and try to enjoy herself; for the very act of riding, even though she was all alone, brought intense pleasure to this girl. She rode fast and daringly. She sat up straight, and dropped the boyish lean that she had affected of late, and which she instinctively felt was a part of what Ethel Garner had meant when she had depreciated her riding. She put her chin on a self-respecting level, her eyes flashing a little defiance as she remembered those girls. She would show them sometime that she also could ride like a lady.

That cut about her riding had gone deeper

than she was willing to acknowledge even to herself, for she was proud of her ability to ride well. She would chew no more gum as she rode, and she would maintain an irreproachable position. Thinking these thoughts, she sped along faster than she realized, and soon had crossed the township road, and was fairly out into the open country. The thought of the party was hateful to her. She tried to live in a world of fancied friends of her own, where she was admired and her company sought after, and where no one spoke of her but to praise. She turned her head slightly and smiled in an imagined talk with a pleasant friend of her own conjuring. Her brown suit became the finest of imported garments. The modest home behind towered into a stately mansion, her mother sat in it at leisure, arrayed in rich silks and costly jewels. The fretful little brother was a lovely child with a French nurse, and there were no more cares or troubles or disagreeable things in her joyful life. Naturally, surrounded by such an atmosphere, she was sweet and lovely herself. Not that Effie had ever sat down and charged her own faults to her surroundings, but her inference was that one who had everything lovely about one could but be lovely one's self. At least, she would for one afternoon be that ideal person, and have things just as she pleased. She even met the other riding party in fancy, and had them look at her with envy and call to her to join them, while she pursued the even tenor of her way, sorry for them that they had to be disappointed, but altogether so engaged with these other and worthier friends of hers that she scarcely remembered that they had passed, five minutes after.

Even the young man, Lawrence Earle, came into the story, as she in imagination gave him a distant nod in response to his eager greeting of open admiration.

Thus drenching her bruised spirit in the healing uplift of her own imaginings she sailed out into a day that was perfect as any June day could be. The sky was blue without a sign of cloud. The blossoms here and there, all the way from dandelion to wild grape were filling the air with sweetness, and the birds were fairly crazy with song, pouring it out into the air like living visible gold. As she rode along her spirit rose to meet the day, and more and more the sorrows of her life dropped away and left her free. She was like a butterfly skimming the golden sunshine, a bird on the wing, as lithe and happy, so happy she could almost burst into song herself.

She tried it a little in a clear throaty contralto, humming a song the boys sang at school. She forgot she was ugly and unwanted, forgot there were excursions from which she was excluded, forgot there were obnoxious young snobs from college who laughed at little tomboys with holes in their skirts and sweaters, forgot that there was anything in this world but free air and sunshine and happiness. In short she was just the little careless Effie again as she had been before she heard those hateful girls down behind the privet hedge in her own side yard.

She whizzed past a farmhouse with three old ladies sitting knitting on the porch and was gone before they discovered she was a girl and not a boy, she shied around a red rooster that was strutting in the road; she flashed by a great dog who was lying in wait to bark at her and chase her, as she pedalled up a long slow hill with the ease of a bird on wing, coasting down again with a broad sweep of meadow and the crossroads ahead of her.

Then suddenly her golden visions vanished and she was hurled back into her hateful world of self-consciousness again. For there ahead of her she saw a shining new car, halting at the crossroads, as if its driver were uncertain which road to take, and another glance at him showed something familiar about the set of his shoulders. Was it, could it be that that was Lawrence Earle? And he had missed the way of course. He had proably meant to join the party on the pike, and missed them, or perhaps they had not carefully outlined their route to him.

She knew perfectly which way they intended to take. She had heard it talked about when she was behind the Garners' hedge, and by Eleanor at the dinner table. If this had been any one else in the world, or any other party of excursionists that he was intending to join, Effie would not have hesitated an instant. She would have ridden with all her might and reached him and told him where he ought to go, that he should turn back at once and take the crossroad to the pike three miles back.

But this was not the usual Effie. This was an awakening girl with a fierce grievance and a heart full of bitterness. What? Warn this young man that he was going away from the rendezvous? Never! She would sooner do anything than that. Help those

58

hateful girls and that supercilious young man who had made fun of her once to come together and have a good time? Not if it were to pour the largest, hottest coals of fire on their heads! She would glory in their separation. It served them right. And there settled down over her a sense of satisfaction that there was an occasional balancing of punishments in this world, and those girls were getting one now. Nevertheless, it made her a little uncomfortable when she looked back to see Mr. Earle riding along on the road she had taken, getting farther and farther away from where he was supposed to want to go, when a word from her might set him right. He would probably pass her in a moment so she concluded to put him out of mind by putting him out of sight, and setting spurs to her steed, she wheeled sharply into a road at the right, level as a table, and tried to rejoice in her sense of freedom. Let him go on and lose his way. It was nothing to her!

Suddenly she became aware that for some minutes there had been a sound of rapid hoofs behind her but she had been enjoying herself too much to pay heed to them. Now as the sounds drew nearer, and she turned her head to see who was driving so madly, she saw it was a grocery wagon, driverless, coming at full speed, the horse apparently almost beside himself with fear, the lines flying in the wind, and its only occupant a little fair-haired child, a tiny boy with golden curls blowing in the breeze, too young to understand, and just old enough to cling to the seat and be frightened. It was a miracle that he had not been thrown out on the hard macadam some distance back. In a moment more that horse would pass her. Instinctively she swerved aside to be out of his way. And now he had passed her, and the blue-eyed baby looked at her and gave a little cry and a beseeching look, and it made her think of her own baby brother's face when he was frightened or hurt. Just ahead, a quarter of a mile, was a sharp turn and a steep hill with a great yawning quarry hole at one side. The baby would be almost certain to be thrown out there, and there was scarcely a chance of any rescue, unless—oh, could she? With a thought of whether she had a right to risk so much when she had so little power to help, she put all her strength to her wheel and shot on down the road after the horse. She could easily outdistance him in a moment or two if she tried, and then—but there was no time for thought—

she *must* ride alongside and catch the bridle or the reins, or something, and stop that horse. She must, or the baby would be killed, and if she did not try she would all her life feel responsible for his life. Not that she really thought this out. It might be said to have flashed through her brain. She acted. Quick as light flashes so her wheel obeyed her motion. She leaned forward now with all her might to get the greatest power and make the quickest time, with no more thought of trying to ride in a ladylike position. She wished she were a man. She wished a man were here to act instead of herself, and so increase the chance of saving the baby. She saw no man ahead now, and thought of the one she had just passed, and wished he were there, for maybe he could help. She forgot that she had just been hating him. She forgot everything but just what she was doing, and then as quick as thought she was beside the foaming horse, wheeling steadily step by step abreast of him, and making ready for her next move. Now her boyish practice of riding this way and that, standing on one pedal or on the saddle, riding on the front and the back and the side, and every other part of her wheel, stood her in good stead. Just how she did it she could not tell afterward; but she caught that horse by the bit and held him for one long, awful, rushing minute, when everything in the world she had ever done passed over her head in clear sequence, and she felt that the end had come. She heard a car coming. Would it be too late? The horse was rearing and plunging again. Could she possibly hold out till some one came? Then a strong hand was placed firmly over hers, and a steady voice said, "Whoa, now, whoa! Steady, boy, steady!" and the horse gradually slackened his pace, and she caught a glimpse of the golden-haired baby still clinging to the seat. She dropped in a little heap somewhere in the road not far from her wheel, and everything grew black and still about her.

Chapter Five

LAWRENCE EARLE was one of the most admired and envied young men in the town. Since he had been a little child playing in the yard of his father's beautiful home, people had watched him and pointed him out and said: "See, that is Lawrence Earle. His father is the wealthiest man in this part of the country, and his mother is one of the very finest women you will find. She is beautiful and dresses like a flower, and has everything that heart could wish, that money can buy, and yet she is just as sweet and gracious and good as if she had nothing to make her proud."

Lawrence did not grow up behind stone walls, and high hedges, too good to have anything to do with the other boys. He went to the public school and took his place with the rest. He played baseball better than any one else in his class, they used to say even when he was in the primary grades. He could swim and climb anything, and he could fight if it became necessary to set something right.

But Lawrence Earle had always stood for fine things. He was always on the level, honest even if it went against him to be, and the boys said he was so square that he couldn't be any squarer.

He stood high in his classes in spite of the fact that he went out for athletics and was always ready for fun. While he was in grammar school and high school his house was always the centre of all the school social doings, and his mother always ready to help in any sudden party or picnic proposed. She was one of them, "a good scout" they used to call her. The boys adored her, and girls admired her and tried to imitate her.

One of the nicest features of these social affairs was that there were no class distinctions; all, whether rich or poor, were welcomed alike.

But when Lawrence went away to college, these social affairs at the Earle home largely ceased. Nearly all of Lawrence's intimate friends were also away at college or gone to work somewhere. Therefore it was that the younger set of whom the Garner girls and Eleanor Martin were members, knew Lawrence and his famous good times only afar. They had been the little children when Lawrence was growing up.

When, therefore, it began to be noised abroad that Lawrence was graduated and would be coming home in a few days all the younger set, who now considered themselves "the" set, began to scheme how they might get hold of him, for they longed to experience for themselves some of those wonderful good times that they had heard their older brothers and sisters talk about.

Lawrence had gained distinction in college, of course, and the news of his successes had drifted home in one way or another. Several of the town boys were in the same college with him, and there was no lack of knowledge concerning his attainments and successes.

Football, basket ball, baseball and scholarship alike seemed to claim him as a hero. The scores he made as captain of this team and that were watched in the papers. When he made Phi Beta Kappa there was a long article about it in the town paper and everybody who had any acquaintance whatever with him or his family spoke of it to everybody else and said how nice it was and that it was of course to have been expected of a boy like Lawrence. In fact, there were no other boys just like Lawrence, they all agreed.

In short Lawrence was in a fair way to have his head turned, and a stranger hearing all his praises sounded would have been likely to feel that Lawrence Earle was a most spoiled, conceited, impossible youth. He was rich and good-looking and smart. What more could a young man have?

But Lawrence Earle had a sensible mother who had early taught him that nothing he had was really his own, only a gift from God, to be most carefully and generously used else it might be taken from him. And

65

as he grew up he showed that he had not a grain of selfishness or conceit in him.

Yet in spite of what he had been, the friends and neighbors who had watched him grow up and learned to love and admire him watched for his home-coming with fear and trembling. For how could it be that a boy with as many things to make him proud as this one, could possibly go through college with such honors as he had won, and not grow proud at least to some extent?

Speculation was rife among the elders. What would the young man do when he came back with his education completed? Would he study law and accept a partnership with his uncle who was somewhat famous as a lawyer in that region? Would he take up a business career as his wealthy father had done? Or would he have a line of his own, journalism perhaps, or philosophy, or art? Every one was interested and wondering.

But the young girls were all in a flutter to get him to their parties, and Eleanor Martin secretly took a few lessons in dancing, though her father and mother did not approve of that amusement, in order that she might not appear awkward before this elegant stranger when he should return and invite them all to his parties perhaps.

But Lawrence Earle rode into town late in the evening in his own car, and drove quietly up to his mother's door, and made no fuss at all about his home-coming. And when he found on the desk in his old room a pile of invitations, he swept them all aside and said,

"Mother, I don't have to go to any of these things just yet, do I? I'm bored to death with functions. I just want to spend a little quiet time with you for a few days before I see anyone, can't I?"

And his mother, with a light in her eyes, smiled and assented.

"Dear, it's to be just as you want it. If you have any friends you want they'll be welcome as always; but it will be my greatest joy to have you all to myself for a while if that will please you best."

"Suits me to a T, Mother dear! I want to take you off on one or two long drives and we'll have a smashing old-time picnic all by ourselves like we used to when I was a little kid. I need that to get back to living again. And besides I've a lot of things to tell you that have developed this year and I hadn't time to write. We've got to have a little leisure for this. About the middle of next week Jimmy and Bryan will come on for a few days, on their way to India. I must tell you all about them. They're great! You'll like 'em. And Ted will run down for a few days and we'll have to get some of the boys together to meet him, but aside from that I've no plans. If you have I'm perfectly willing, only wait a few days, won't you, so I can get my bearings?"

His mother smiled, the glad light growing in her eyes. Her boy was unchanged, unspoiled. She held her head proudly.

"There aren't many of the old crowd left, are there? Sam Jones and the Mills boys are down at the foundry, you said, and Fetler is married. Poor little fish! Why didn't he wait till he had enough money to support a wife? And Cappellar is in California, and Jarvis is gone to New York to study medicine, and Butler and Williams went to South America, and Judson is dead. That only leaves Brown and Tommy Moore and the Ellsworths of my class, doesn't it? I was counting them up on my way home. Not many for a reunion."

"You don't say anything about the girls!" suggested his mother.

"Oh, the girls! Well there weren't so many

68

of them that mattered. Margaret Martin is married, you wrote. I hope she got a good man. She certainly was a peach of a girl! And Wilda Hadley eloped. She always was a fool. Lilly Garner married too, didn't she? Lives in New York, you said. What became of Evelyn Bradley? She was the prettiest girl in the class, and knew it too, didn't she? Remember the time I caught her posing before that mirror at our senior class party?"

"Evelyn is out in Hollywood in the movies," said Mrs. Earle a little sadly. "It was a great disappointment to her mother. She tried to keep her at home. Evelyn has a younger sister now who is even prettier than she was. Don't you remember Maud, a little bit of a black-eyed girl with soft black curls?"

"Can't say I do," answered Lawrence. "I suppose all those babies have grown up, haven't they?"

"Yes," smiled his mother, "it is the babies that were then who are inviting you now. I think Maud is one of those girls in that picnic to-morrow. They came here to ask me if I thought you would come, and I promised to tell you all about it. The Garner girls, and Eleanor Martin and Janet Chipley and a new girl, Cornelia Gilson, very modern with glorious red hair. I'm not sure that

I admire her type. Oh, you wouldn't know the parties nowadays, Lawrence! They're nothing like the good times you used to have here at home. Why they wouldn't be satisfied three minutes with the games you used to play and have such grand times with. They've got to dance, dance, dance, and flirt, "petting" they call it now. My dear! But you haven't lived out of the world, Son; you know what life is now."

"Yes, I've lived out of it a good deal, Mother, though I know what you mean. I had sort of hoped it wouldn't have penetrated to our town yet but I suppose that wasn't to be expected. But if it's like that here too we'll just cut it out. I haven't any use at all for it. Will you make my excuses to those girls Mother, or shall I have to write?"

"I suppose you had better write a note, Son. But even then they may come down upon you and carry you off. They are perfectly crazy to have you go on this excursion. They have been planning it for days and arranged the time with special view to your being here."

"Well, I can't help it, I'm not going!" said Lawrence with a firm set of his jaw. "I hate that sort of thing anyway. Why

70

shouldn't you and I run off for a day, take a drive to Aunt Lila's or something, and don't return till the blamed thing is over?"

"I'd love to," said the mother, "but unfortunately I've got a meeting for that day, the Mite Society, and it's away out in the country at old Mrs. Petrie's. You remember her? She is lame and blind and the ladies are going out there to give her a little pleasure as she can't come in to the meetings any more. I'd get out of it if I hadn't promised to take Mrs. Mason's place leading the devotional, and then I'm also chairman of the refreshment committee and have to look after the luncheon, and in the afternoon we're going to present Mrs. Petrie with a little purse, and they've asked me to make the speech."

"Well, of course you've got to go. I'll drive you over. How'll that be? And then I'll take a run around to all my old haunts, and come back for you in the afternoon? What time do you go?"

"The meeting starts at half past ten, and it isn't over till three. I'm afraid you'll get tired travelling around all that time. Why not come back to lunch with us? Mrs. Petrie would be delighted, and so would all the old

71

ladies, and your mother would certainly be proud to show you off to her old friends."

"Well, I might if I get around. I'll see. So that's settled. But how about getting off early in the morning before anybody can possibly come around or call up or anything. Wouldn't you enjoy a ride out to the Rocks, say, before you go to Petrie's?"

"I certainly would. How ideal! I feel like a girl again with my best boy going to take me out." And Mrs. Earle stooped and kissed the handsome brow of her son tenderly. "Dear son! It's so good to have you home again!"

So Lawrence wrote his note and posted it by special delivery, and when Maud Bradley called up in the morning to present a few added attractions and beseech him to reconsider, Lawrence Earle and his mother were driving along the highway at a joyous speed, bound for old Mother Petrie's, via "the Rocks," with an ice-cream freezer, two cake boxes, and a big basket of sandwiches stowed in the tonneau of the car.

"It's just too provoking for anything!" said Maud explaining it to the Garner girls over the telephone. "There I went and made an extra angel cake just for him, and I sat up almost all night to finish the embroidery on my new dress! They say he is just the same as he used to be but I don't believe it. He's a snob. He thinks we're too young for his Royal Highness! But I mean to drag him into our set yet. Mamma's going to invite him over to dinner Saturday night. She says he used to be real intimate with Evelyn when they were in school together. We'll get him yet, and then we'll have another of these picnics, won't we?"

"I suppose he thinks we're too small potatoes," said Ethel. "But when he learns how speedy we can be he'll sit up and take notice. Never mind, Bradley, he'll come next time. Wait till he hears all we do on this trip. I'll take measures to have his mother hear all about it. Aunt Beth runs in there often to see her, and Aunt Beth will tell her all about it. By the way, you knew Eleanor was going to be allowed to take her new car, didn't you? Well, I planned you and the Hall boys and Joe Whiting and Aline would go with her; Minturn too can squeeze in if he doesn't get his own car from the repair shop in time. Reitha and Betty Anne are going with Sam and Fred, and the Loring boys and Jessie Heath will go with us. But it does seem as if half the day was spoiled without Lawrence Earle, doesn't it? When we've counted so on his going, too! Isn't it hateful?"

"Yes, it is," gloomed Maud. "If I had known he wasn't going I wouldn't have tried to finish that dress, and I'd have had some sleep. As it is I shall just have a miserable headache all day long and all for nothing."

"Well, you got your dress finished, didn't you? You can be glad of that much."

"Yes, but what's the use? The other boys never notice what you have on. All they want is something to eat at a picnic."

"Well, give them your angel cake and forget it," laughed Ethel. "We'll have a good time any way, and just remember to be thankful that we didn't have to cart that disagreeable Effie Martin along. If Lawrence Earle had gone with us and she had been along I'd have died of mortification to have him think she was one of us."

"Yes, so should I. You'd better keep Flora away from her vicinity next time. Flora is too soft-hearted."

"Well, I've fixed her. She knows what to say the next time Effie Martin asks her for an invitation. I made her understand that we don't want to be mixed up at any time with a girl who has a reputation like Effie's! Well, good-bye, I've got to finish putting

74

the salts and peppers and olives and things in. Don't forget the paper plates and napkins." Maud hung up the receiver with a sigh.

Chapter Six

THE fresh, bracing air and the relaxed position soon brought Effie back to consciousness. At first she was just a little bewildered at her surroundings, for in that brief interval of unconsciousness she had thought herself lying in her mother's armchair at home and listening to her mother's sweet voice saying, "My little Euphemia."

She had never liked her name. It was so queer and old-fashioned, just like the aunt for whom she had been named, but now in her mother's tones, with that note of pleased surprise in her appearance, she was conscious as she returned to life again that the name sounded pleasant.

Then the scene was suddenly changed and she lay in the road with a group of curious strangers about her, and heard a strong voice, that same voice that had spoken to the horse in such commanding tones, say, "Raise her head a little. There! She is opening her eyes. Now, where is that cup of water?" She looked up and saw Lawrence Earle bending anxiously over her.

With her constitutional impulsiveness she sat up, told them she was all right, and then jumped to her feet, but found she was more unstrung than she knew by her faint, for she tottered and would have fallen again had not Earle reached out a strong arm and supported her. He made her sit down on the bank a few minutes and some one brought her a tin cup of water from a wayside spring. Effie felt very much astonished, for she could not remember to have been of so much importance since she had the scarlet fever many years ago and her mother had given up everything else and ministered to her.

At first she sat on the grass, dazed, not really understanding what had happened, but by degrees her memory returned, and she began to realize what she had been through. Then she started up and asked anxiously:

"Where is the kid? Is he all right?"

"All right," said the young man soothingly as if she were a sick baby. "The woman in the farmhouse took him in to give him a drink of milk. He was only badly frightened. But if he had gone on a few rods farther nothing could have prevented a catastrophe. You saved the child's life. The quarry hole is just ahead—"

"I know," murmured Effie as if she were remembering a story she had read. "That's why I jumped at him just then."

"Well, you certainly did just the right thing!" said Earle heartily. "I never saw a rescue more neatly made. You hurled yourself at that horse as if you had been doing it every day of your life. You certainly had your courage with you all right! Some girl, I should say!"

Effie's cheeks suddenly flushed red with consciousness:

"Oh that wasn't anything!" she said almost sullenly, her eyes clouding over with bitterness as she remembered the day and why she was off here riding alone when she would much rather have been on an excursion with the other girls.

"Well, I guess you'll find that kid's parents will think it is something when they get here," said Earle earnestly. "Why that baby would be lying down in the quarry hole now if it hadn't been for you. They say a big rock has fallen from the bank this side of the road, and there wouldn't have been room for the wagon to pass if the horse had tried to go through. It would have been certain death for the child if you hadn't saved him!"

"Well, there wasn't anybody else to do it," said Effie. "I had to do my best." Her voice was still bitterly gloomy.

"Well, you did it all right, and you're a heroine, though you don't seem to know it yet," smiled the young man.

"Humph!" said Effie scornfully, "people don't make heroines out of my kind of stuff. You'll find out. They'll simply say I'm an awful tomboy and I ought to have stood back and waited for some man to take care of the kid. I know. I've heard 'em before!"

A rush of sudden tears came surprisingly into Effie's eyes. She wasn't a girl given to crying in public, but the shock of her recent experience had shaken her up. She brushed the tears away angrily, and jerked herself up from the bank.

"Where's my bicycle?" she asked roughly as a small boy might have done. "I gotta get out of here before anybody comes around. I'll never hear the last of this. And I've torn my new dress, too!" she ended helplessly, looking ruefully down at a jagged tear under one of the pleats.

"You should worry," said the young man

lightly. "You saved the kid's life. There are more dresses in the world, but you can't get a new child to take the place of one you love. You sit down again. You aren't fit to start out yet. You've had a shock and must rest."

"Aw rats!" said Effie inelegantly, relapsing into her boy vernacular, "I'm no baby doll. Where's my wheel?"

"Your wheel is pretty badly damaged," he told her gently. "The wagon wheel ran over it when you dropped it, and the horse kicked it and stepped on it once or twice, but I think it can be put in shape. However, don't you realize that doesn't matter? There are also other wheels in the world."

"Not for me!" snapped Effie. "This was my new wheel. I bought it myself with money I had saved up. Where is it? I've got to get away from here."

"Look here, sister, I'm here to take care of you just now, and you've got to sit and rest till the doctor gets here and I'm sure you're all right. You don't seem to know it, but you had a narrow escape yourself. That horse came within an inch of kicking you in the temple when you fell, after I took hold of him, and I'm going to make sure you were not injured before you start home if I have to bind you hand and foot to do it. Now will you be a good child? Look here, what's your name? I think we ought to notify your folks that you're all right, don't you? Bad news travels fast. They may be worrying about you."

"Nobody ever worries about me," said Effie petulantly. "They expect me to do crazy things. They're ashamed of me for doing them. They say I'm too big to ride a bicycle."

"Well, this morning's work is nothing to be ashamed of, I'll testify, and I'm not so sure you're correct about their not worrying. People sometimes worry a lot and never say anything about it. As soon as the doctor gets here and the kid's parents come to take him home I'm going to bundle you into my car, wheel and all, and take you home too. We'll leave your wheel at the best repair shop in town, and I'll promise you it will come back to you in a day or two as good as new."

Effie looked at him half belligerently a moment and then said, somewhat ungraciously:

"Thanks, but you needn't bother with me. I can walk home and wheel my bicycle myself. You ought to be on your way. Mr.

Earle, they've gone over the township road. You must have passed it three miles back and missed your way. I might have told you before, I suppose. I saw you back at the crossroads. But if you hurry you can catch them. They'll probably wait for you till the last minute, and they'll be awfully disappointed if you don't get there. They're counting on you, and I'm sure I don't want to spoil their pleasure. It won't make things any better for me to have them have a horrid time."

The young man stared at her in astonishment:

"I beg your pardon," he said in a puzzled tone. "You seem to have the advantage of me. I've been away so much that you girls have grown out of all recognition, although I've thought there was something familiar about you from the first. Who are you, please?"

"You won't know any better when I tell you," she snapped, "and you better get on as fast as you can, for the girls will be frightfully angry at me if they find out I was what kept you and made you late."

"Made me late? What can you mean? Won't you explain, please? I'm not aware I'm late for anything. I was just riding around looking over my old haunts, with half the day before me and nothing to do."

"But weren't you going on the picnic with the girls and boys?" asked Effie perplexed. "Perhaps you've got the dates mixed. I know you were going, for I heard the girls talking about it. They fixed the date so you would be home. The Garner girls and Maud Bradley, you know."

Effie was talking earnestly now, like a girl who was trying to do her duty at last and meant to do it thoroughly even though it cost her everything.

Lawrence Earle smiled:

"No," he said, showing all his white teeth gleefully. "No, you're all wrong. I wasn't going on that excursion. I declined. I wanted the day to do as I pleased. I wasn't ready to go out into society yet. But you're awfully kind to try to set me right. I appreciate that part of it."

"I'm not kind at all," said Effie crossly, feeling a queer lump in her throat. "I didn't want to tell you, at all. I wanted you to get lost and them to be disappointed. But, of course that wasn't right."

The young man regarded her amusedly.

"And may I ask why you wanted them to be disappointed?" he inquired. "There seems to be something interesting back of all this. Perhaps we're comrades in guilt, who knows? Because I'm not conscious of caring much myself whether they are disappointed or not. They're all strangers to me. Come, tell me why you wanted them to be disappointed."

Nobody had ever coaxed Effie in this pleasant merry way before. She scarcely understood such treatment. She swept him a searching glance to see if he was kidding her.

"Tell me!" he urged in a kindly tone.

"Because they didn't want me to go along," she blurted out at last!

"Oh!" said the young man with twinkling eyes, "so, that's what's the matter! Well, I think they showed very poor taste indeed, myself. Tell me about it."

He dropped down on the grass by her side and began to pull long dandelions and split up their pale-green luscious stems into two neat ringlets.

But Effie felt a sudden rush of dumbness come over her. There was something in his kindly comradeship which choked her and made words impossible. She did not remember ever to have had any one talk to her in this friendly confidential manner. It fairly overwhelmed her.

He watched her quietly for a moment, saw that for some reason she could not talk about it, and then went on in the same even pleasant tone.

"First, tell me who you are. I'm sure I ought to know you. You still seem somehow strangely familiar."

Then words rushed to Effie's lips:

"No, you don't know me. At least you wouldn't remember me. The last time you saw me you laughed at me."

The quick color sprang to the young man's cheeks:

"Oh, surely not!" he exclaimed. "Aren't you mistaken? Perhaps you misunderstood. I'm sure I never meant to.'"

"No, I didn't misunderstand," said Effie bitterly. "All the girls said you did, and I remembered it too when I heard them talk about it. But you did have a reason of course. I had torn my dress and your mother told me about it and I said I knew it, that it was too much trouble to mend it when I was off at the seashore."

Light broke on the young man's face.

"Oh, you're the kid that was having such a good time with Tommy Moore, aren't you? I remember. Why, kid, I wasn't laughing *at* you; I was laughing *with* you, didn't you know that? I thought it was refreshing to see a real girl once more after the specimens of painted dolls I had been talking with. For a fact I came near throwing down my hat and joining in your game of tag. If it hadn't been that I was taking Mother to call on an old friend who was leaving that night I believe I would, if for nothing else than to shock that Bradley girl. I detest her! I've watched her and her sister grow up and they're the most artificial girls I ever saw. I enjoyed you because you were so happy and spontaneous."

"But I wasn't a bit polite," said Effie reluctantly. "I was rude and unmannerly. The girls said so. They said I was a flat tire, and all sorts of things and of course I knew it was true, only it made me mad for them to say so, and not to want me on the ride. I didn't want to go for their sake. I can't bear them, they're so stuck-up and silly about boys. And I didn't want to go to be on their old picnic either, but I did want to drive the car part way. Father said I might, and I wanted to, and it would have been fun."

"Of course, it would, but there are lots of other chances to drive cars and if I were you

I wouldn't have a regret about that picnic. For my part I'm having a better time right here and now than if I had gone. I wouldn't have missed seeing that rescue this morning for worlds."

Effie flashed him a look of wonder and sudden joy. Could anybody say a thing like that to her and really mean it? He must be only meaning to be polite.

"But you know you haven't told me your name yet. Aren't you going to? I suppose I should remember which one you were from the last time I saw you, but I hadn't paid the slightest attention to any of their names. The only girl I was sure of was that Bradley girl and I didn't know which one she was for sure."

Effie's flash of joy vanished into her habitual gloom:

"Well, you wouldn't have remembered it if you had heard it, and I don't think anybody mentioned it that day. It wasn't thought necessary. I'm only Effie Martin, the girl that nobody likes."

"Well, that's not true," said Earle heartily, "for I like you. Even seeing you just this morning I can't help liking you, and why shouldn't everybody else? But say— why—you can't be the little Euphemia—

86

Margaret Martin's little sister, that I taught to pitch a ball, can you? Say, now, I believe you are!"

Effie's face lit up with a glow that made it almost beautiful, and she nodded, shyly, wistfully:

"Sure!" she admitted almost embarrassedly. Her mother wouldn't have known her by her manner at all, it was so sweet and shy and pleased.

"Well, now this is great!" said Earle. "I can see that you and I are going to be great friends. I always liked your sister Margaret better than any of the other girls. They tell me she has got married. You must miss her, don't you? But say, this is going to be fine! Can you pitch a ball yet?"

Effie dropped her eyelashes ashamed.

"Yes," she admitted. "But they make a lot of fun of me. They call me a tomboy and say I'm too old for things like that!"

"Nonsense!" said Earle! "Bologny! We'll teach them better. Let's make it the fashion to pitch ball, and then we'll see all those girls out in their back yards practising. When can I come over and have a game of ball with you? I want to see how you have progressed. You were wonderful as a child, and I'll bet you have become a pippin at it. Say, do you know I never forgot you. I remember finding the meaning of your name one day when I was studying. Do you know what it means? Euphemia?"

"No," said Effie shortly. "I only know I hate it. I wish I had a decent name. Everybody makes fun of it."

"Oh, but they oughtn't. Euphemia means 'Of good report.' It bears a recommendation on the surface, you see. Your very name is a good reference."

Euphemia was still for a moment and then she said:

"Well, it doesn't fit me." She said it so bitterly that the young man yearned to help her.

"Make it fit then," he said earnestly.

"How?" she asked with an eagerness that showed she had asked that question in her thoughts before.

He was silent for an instant:

"Whatsoever things are true, whatsoever things are honest, whatsoever things are just—" he quoted, "whatsoever things are pure, whatsoever things are lovely, whatsoever things are of good report; if there be any virtue, and if there be any praise, think on these things."

He was still for a minute and then he added:

"There is One who will help you in that, Euphemia. I wonder if you have Him for your Friend and Savior? He is mine, and He is able to help in everything like that. I know, for I've tried it."

"Oh, but you've never been disagreeable as they say I am!"

He flashed her a look of sympathy:

"Euphemia you don't know what I've been. But anyhow that doesn't make any difference. He's able to keep us from any kind of falling, if we let Him. We'll talk about this some time again if you will. There's a lot I would like to tell you. I see a car coming now. I think the doctor is here. Would you like to go up to the house, or shall we stay right here?"

Chapter Seven

EVENTUALLY they got into the big car that drew up in front of them, and rode with the doctor into the driveway and up to the big old farmhouse, where the little runaway boy was having the time of his life chasing a lot of downy yellow chickens.

89

The grocer boy was there, much disturbed, shouting an account of the affair over the telephone to his employers. It appeared that he had arrived on a motor-cycle while Effie was still unconscious, having requisitioned the motor-cycle to chase his horse. The owner of the motor-cycle was there too, enjoying the general excitement, and eating gingerbread and milk. The farmer's sons were there outside the door, rubbing down the excited horse after the most approved method, talking wisely about horseflesh in general, and this thin old cranky grocer's horse in particular. The farmer's wife was there, petting the beautiful little boy and telling him his mamma was coming right away. And the horse was there, still snuffing and snorting occasionally, giving furtive side glances and sidestepping himself with nervous jumps at each little sound or movement, rolling the whites of his eyes wickedly, and lifting his velvety lips with a snarl to show his great yellow teeth.

The grocer's boy at the telephone was telling his story in loud tones:

"You see how 'tis, I was up ta Harrisses waitin' fer the check as you tol' me, an' the kid clumb in the wagon. He often does.

He's allus crazy ta ride when I go up there, an' I kid him a lot. Wha's that? No sir. I didn't let him get in. No sir, I don't never 'low him ta get in. I ain't got tha time. No sir, he jus' clumb in of hisself after I was gone in the house, see? Yessir, I was standin' right where I could see the wagon, an' I called to the kid ta get out, see? But he jus' laughed and kep a-jerkin' the reins, an' jus' then the missus she sent down the check, an' I heard a car come up. It was a d'livery truck, ice, er somethin', an' it made a big noise, an' had some queer kinda horn, an' it blew it right in that hoss's ear, an' she ups and clips it. I knowed what would happen when I see that car a-comin' an' I flew down them steps, yessir, but I couldn't get a holt of the lines, they was on the other side of her, an' she was makin' fer round the house and down through the other gateway, so I turns around to head her off at the front, but they was diggin' some kind of a ditch fer a drain pipe, or a water pipe or a gas pipe, or somethin' an' I fell plumb in an almos' broke my ankle, and stunned myself, so when I got up that there hoss was dashing outta the front gate, an' up the road, an' I hadn't got no chancet, see? Yessir, I know. Yessir, I did. I saw a feller comin' on a motor bike, an' I hailed him an' he brung me along. An' I got here almos' as soon ez she did, but some plucky girl on a bike had stopped the hoss. Yessir. No sir, the kid ain't hurt none, jus' scared. Yessir he's playin' about big as life. Yessir. The doctor's come an' says he's all right. No sir, the mother ain't come yet but she'll be here in a minute. Yessir, I will. I'll come along back as soon as she gets here. Yessir, the meat's all delivered 'cept Mrs. Buckingham's over on the pike, an' she won't kick, she's a lady, she is. Yessir! All right, sir. Goodbye!"

Effie took the doctor's examination of her with something of resentment. Of course there was nothing the matter with her, but she submitted to having her pulse taken, and her heart listened to with something of her old belligerent air. It was only when Earle smiled at her that she lost her strained attitude and relaxed into a normal creature; her face lit up once more with that sweet wonder that anybody should care to be so nice and pleasant to her, and she remembered the wonderful words her new friend had just repeated, with something like a thrill in her heart. Was this going to be a way out of her difficulty, she wondered? It sounded unpractical, but it also sounded beautiful—"Think on these things"—It was something to hide in her heart and study out anyway. Where did he get those words? They were somewhere in the Bible, she felt sure. It seemed as if she could remember her Sunday school class droning the verse out in concert some time back through the years, but she couldn't be sure. They were strangely familiar, yet she never remembered to have thought they meant anything in particular before.

But another surprise was in store for Effie. Another great car presently drew up before the farmhouse steps, driven by a liveried chauffeur. A slim stylish lady in beautiful black satin, with a long string of pearls around her neck, got out and rushed at the little boy.

She held the child in a long embrace, and when she finally put him down and turned back to speak to them all, there were tears on her face and she was white around her mouth.

"Where is the girl who saved my son's life?" she asked, searching the group with the bluest eyes Effie thought she had ever seen.

And then she rushed at Effie and kissed

her, and Effie felt as if an angel had touched her. Such soft lips, like Mother's only softer and younger. Such delicate perfume like violets! Such a sweet voice. Effie was thrilled again. What wonderful things were happening to her all at once.

"Why, I didn't do anything at all," stammered Effie, honest and frank as ever. "I only held on till Mr. Earle came. He really did it, you know."

But the lady only said: "Oh, you dear child! But suppose you hadn't held on!" and then she kissed Effie and cried again, and after that she turned around and tried to thank Lawrence Earle, and cried some more. Effie stood in awe and wondered what all those girls who had criticized her would think if they knew where she was now. They would likely blame her somehow for being there. And then and there she resolved that they should never know if she could help it.

Then the whirl and excitement of it all began to make her feel sick and giddy, and all at once she found Lawrence Earle's eyes upon her, and he said very pleasantly that he really must take Miss Martin home now, and unless there was something else he could do they would go at once.

All at once the bottom seemed to have dropped out of things for Effie. She began to look around for Miss Martin. Was she then to have no further opportunity to ask her new friend where to find that Bible verse? Most likely she would never see him again either. Somehow the chair by which she was standing seemed to rise up and shake off her unsteady hand, and all the people in the room got dim and misty and whirled into one mass. Then she heard the doctor's voice saying something about more air, and the next thing she knew she was out on the driveway being helped into Lawrence Earle's beautiful car. His arm was around her, and a voice was saying—it was the sweet voice of the baby's mother—"Oh, I do hope she isn't going to suffer any ill effects from this. Are you sure, doctor, that she's all right?"

When they brought the child to say goodbye and thank her she realized they had been talking about her, and she managed to smile in her old swaggering manner and declared there was nothing at all the matter with her.

Out on the road at last she found that her companion was looking at her anxiously.

"You are perfectly sure you are all right?" he asked.

And then she found herself smiling at him.

"Why, yes," she said. "I just felt a little queer in there. I'm all right now I'm out in the air. Isn't this car grand?"

"Do you like it? So do I," he said. "Now will your mother worry if we don't go right home? It's after twelve o'clock and you ought to have something to eat at once. Then you'll feel better. There's a tea room over here a mile or so. Shall we go and get a bite? I'm hungry as a bear myself. I would have urged you to eat something in there when the woman offered it, but I thought it would be better for you to get off where it was quiet to eat. You have been through a lot of excitement, you know."

Effie laughed.

"Why nobody minds how much excitement I go through. That never made any difference with me," she said gaily.

"But you don't make a practice of making flying leaps from bicycles at runaway horses every day, you know, and you did faint clear away, you know, and almost did it again just now."

"Well, I guess that was because I forgot

96

to eat any breakfast," said Effie apologetically. "I was busy, and then I was in a hurry to get away."

"Ah!" said Earle, "I thought you were hungry. Now we'll have some good hot soup and perhaps a cup of tea or coffee, and whatever else we can find. We're out for a good time, you know. Shall I telephone your mother that you won't be home for lunch?"

"Oh no," said Effie in surprise, "they never expect me till I get there. They never worry about me."

"I wouldn't be so sure of that," said Earle looking at her thoughtfully. "People don't always tell all they are feeling, you know. Here's our tea room. Now, do you feel like getting out?"

Effie sprang out quite like her old self, only wondering a little at the gone feeling in her muscles, and the wan feeling around her lips.

She sat at the dainty table in the wayside tea room wondering at herself. To think that she was here being taken to lunch by a young man! What would those hateful girls say if they knew! A pang almost of pity for their disappointment shot through her. They would never forgive her for having the young man they coveted when they could not get

97

him! But of course they need never know. She would tell her mother sometime, perhaps. But it was enough that she should enjoy it all to herself. They would somehow manage to spoil it all for her by some catty remark if they found it out. Why have it desecrated?

So Effie ate her delicious lunch ordered with a view to giving her strength, and enjoyed every mouthful of it, feeling every bit herself when it was finished. Soup and salad and ice cream, delicious tea and delicate crackers with cheese, creamed chicken on toast! Somehow such feasts had seldom come her way, though the home table was abundant and not lacking in modest luxuries on occasion. But this was wonderful! And the feeling of comradeship! It was so new and sweet to the girl that it made her throat sting and her eyes smart to think about it.

After the lunch was over they drove around by a new road that even Effie with her habit of scouring the country on her wheel had not known. It was a crossroad through a lovely wood, with ferns and maidenhair and wild flowers in profusion, as if this was their special secret hiding place from the world, where they only blossomed for God and those who came to seek his special treasures.

They stopped and picked some of them. Effie was laughing and gay and at ease, all the bitterness gone out of her voice, a lilt in it like other girls.

"You don't know how much you are like your sister Margaret," said the young man impulsively as he helped her back into the car again, and his eyes lingered on her face pleasantly bringing the happy color into her cheeks. "Your sister Margaret was one fine girl, I thought," he added earnestly.

Effie looked thoughtful.

"I wish she hadn't got married," she said impulsively. "We always had good times when she was at home. She was the only one who never got impatient with me. She— seemed to understand how I felt."

"She had straight fine brows like yours," mused the young man looking at her again with a pleasant smile. "I think you must be like her."

"Oh, no! I'm not," disclaimed Effie frankly. "I'm not a bit sweet-tempered like her. I get angry and impatient at everything and I'm untidy, and homely, and lazy and selfish. I know, for everybody tells me, and I can see it's true."

"Oh, now look here," said Earle laughing. "That's not the way to give yourself a good report. Don't go to work and blacken your character like that. I don't believe it. See! I know you are not any of those things. I know you are not going to be, either. I can read your character better than that. Besides, you know you can have a Helper any time when you see those tendencies cropping out. He is always ready to help."

"I think you are wonderful!" burst out Effie. "I didn't know young men ever talked like that. What made it? Was it your mother bringing you up that way? I know she is sweet and dear. My mother likes her a lot. But I never heard the other girls tell about your being this way, almost like a minister. They told how you were a great athlete, and had wonderful parties and all sorts of doings at your house and were a wonderful tennis player and awfully kind and all that, but they never said you were—well, this way. I wanted some one to help me awfully, but never would have thought of coming to you. I didn't know young men and boys ever thought much about God."

It was Earle's turn to look thoughtful now.

"You see there is something the matter with my report too, sister," he said at last.

"Oh, no," began Effie deeply chagrined at what she had said. "I didn't mean that. I meant—"

"I know you didn't, little Euphemia," he said gently. "You didn't mean it at all, but it was there all the same. Well, I'll tell you. I guess you never got the report that I was much of a Christian because when these people here knew me I wasn't. That's the truth. I hadn't found God yet. I didn't know that He wanted me to live as close to Him and realize Him as I would an earthly friend. I didn't realize Jesus Christ at all as a factor in my daily life. Oh, I believed what I had been taught that Christ was my Savior from sin in a general way, but I didn't feel much of a sinner, and I didn't spend much of my time thinking about what it meant to have a Savior. Why should I when I didn't realize I needed him? I didn't read the Bible either, very much. Of course I knew a lot of it. Mother saw to that, but it was only in my head, not in my heart. But all that is changed now. Everything is different. Last winter I met Jesus Christ!"

"What do you mean?" asked Effie with bated breath. "How could you meet Him?"

"Do you remember the story of Saul on his way to persecute Christians in Damascus?

Well, it was something like that. Oh, no light or anything. And I wasn't trying to put over anything like a persecution, but I guess I'd been pretty much against a little crowd of fellows in the college whom I used to call fanatics. And then, one night one of them got run down by a truck as he was crossing the road to our car to find out the score on a game we had played, and it fell to my lot to take him back to the dormitory and stay with him all that night while he was dying, and the next day when his folks came, too late. And I tell you I never experienced anything like it. That fellow just lay there in all that terrible suffering and talked to us with his failing strength, told us how great it was to serve his God, and looked death in the face with a smile. I'll never forget it. I saw God with my heart that night, and I resolved I'd try to take his place after he was gone and let my life witness for God the way his had done. It was a great life. It was just Christ living in him!"

Earle was talking now, more as if Effie were an older person and he had to justify himself in her eyes, prove his case, and bring her to see as he saw, and she listened with wonder as to a story in a book that had suddenly walked out and become true.

102

He drew up then in front of a pretty country home, and looked at her.

"I'm due here to get my mother. Do you mind?" he asked with a smile. "I meant to ask if you would rather I took you home first, but we've talked so hard I forgot it."

They had stopped once on their way and left the wheel at a repair shop and had driven on talking so intently that Effie had not noticed which way they were going. Now she started and became instantly self-conscious and uncomfortable.

"Oh, of course not," she stammered, but she did mind exceedingly. To have Earle's beautiful well-bred mother see her here in her son's car, as if she had tried to get his attention! She remembered also the tear in her dress, and tried to smooth it down and cover it up. What would Mrs. Earle think when she found little disreputable Effie Martin riding around with her son? The minute or two that they waited for Mrs. Earle to come out to the car were most painful to the girl, as she sat silent and distraught, wishing she dared climb out and run away. But that was like the old Effie, and she was done with that Effie forever she hoped. The new Euphemia must sit still and face whatever came, and try to be a woman.

She came to herself sufficiently to offer to get into the back seat and let Mrs. Earle occupy the front seat with her son, but the lady declined with the loveliest smile.

"Indeed, no, dear! I always sit in the back seat, and love it. I would rather you sat right still where you are. Besides I have a lot of baskets and things to pile in beside me and must have plenty of room. Lawrence, all those things on the step are to go in. Can you manage to stow them away?"

Then Mrs. Earle leaned forward and asked Effie about her mother and the baby whom she had heard was not well, and Effie found she could open her mouth and speak quite naturally in answer. In a moment more Lawrence had jumped in beside her, slammed the car door shut and they were off again into the sunny afternoon. What a day she had had! She sat still and let the wonder of it roll over her while Mrs. Earle asked her son how he had occupied his time.

"Why, Mother, I ran right into an adventure, as soon as I left you."

"You don't mean it," said his mother in a

voice that entered into her son's adventure with the zest of his own age.

"Yes," he said gaily, "I was hesitating which way to turn when I saw this young lady whirl by on a bicycle, and I was tempted to follow down the road she had taken, for it looked a pleasant way, and the first thing she did was to chase after a runaway horse and save a baby's life, and get herself almost killed in the bargain, and so that was where I came in. We picked ourselves up and got some lunch after a while, and took the bicycle to the repair shop, and here we are. What do you think of Euphemia, Mother? Doesn't she look like her sister Margaret?"

"Why, I believe she does," said Mrs. Earle looking at Effie with the friendliest smile. "I never thought of it before, but she really does."

"Well, you ought to have seen her catch that horse! It was great!"

Effie's cheeks burned with shyness and joy over the kindly words of Mrs. Earle, and she was so pleased and dazed with all their praise that she was quite subdued and sweet when they put her down at her own door. Mrs. Earle said she hoped she would suffer no ill effects from the adventure, and they whirled away.

Effie turned and walked into the house as if she had suddenly stepped out of a dream into reality.

There was no one in sight. Well, then no one had seen her return! That was good. She need not tell any one. She might keep this precious experience to herself, and not have the life of it guyed out of her by the teasing of her family.

She went upstairs to her room, shut and locked the door, and went and stood in front of her mirror looking into her own eyes with steady glance.

"Euphemia," she said slowly, softly, to herself in the glass. "You've got to be different after this. You've got to be of good report." Then she turned and dropped upon her knees beside her bed and prayed, whispering the words in a voice of awe:

"Dear Christ, please do that for me too. Please show me how to be a witness. I want to have you help me."

Chapter Eight

THE famous picnic which had been so carefully planned and eagerly anticipated, was

106

not such a great success as had been expected.

In the first place the guest of honor was not present, the guest for whom Maud Bradley had secretly planned it, though she had not let the girls know she knew he was coming at that time.

Maud had done her best at the last minute to get hold of him in spite of his polite note of refusal. She even went herself to the Earle house as early in the morning as she thought it discreet to appear there, but found to her dismay that both Lawrence and his mother were gone for the day. That alone was enough to spoil the party for Maud, for she had laid her plans so that she might hope to retain the young man for her own especial escort. In fact there was not one girl in the bunch with the possible exception of Flora Garner, who was not in some form or other cherishing some quiet plan to take possession of the guest of the day as her own private property. Even Eleanor Martin had decided to make much of Lawrence Earle's former friendship for her older sister Margaret in order to claim his attention. It was a great thing for the whole crowd to have the young man back at home after his long absence, and the halo that surrounded his reputation made him the more desirable.

When, therefore, the company gathered car by car, and the news was broken to each one that Lawrence Earle would not be with them that day, there was dire dismay. Several girls, against the advice of their mothers, had worn their best dresses, with the young stranger especially in mind, and these looked down at their crisp new frocks in dismay, for there was no denying the wisdom of the mother's sage advice. The dresses would never be so fresh and pretty again after a day of frolicking, part of the time in the woods and part of the time crowded into automobiles. And now there would be no fresh frock for the next occasion when the young man might be more gracious.

Janet Chipley even went so far as to try and get her carload to turn back to her home on the pretext of having forgotten a box of mints, thinking to slip upstairs and make a change in her garments while they waited. But the driver of her car persuaded her otherwise, and the day began with a number of girls being much upset in temper.

This attitude on the part of the girls gradually had its effect on the boys of the party.

"Oh, Jan, give us a rest on Earle, we're sick of his name. What's he anyway? He doesn't belong to our crowd. Forget it. I'm glad he didn't come. You girls wouldn't have had eyes for anybody else. He's nothing so great anyway! Other men have made Phi Beta Kappa. Other men have been captains of teams and nines, and won honors. For Pete's sake forget him and pass the sandwiches!"

Then they had taken the wrong road, and turning back failed to find the charming picnic spot they had started for, or the spring where they expected to drink.

There was salt in the ice cream, and some one had forgotten to bring sugar for the thermos bottles of hot coffee. Jessie Heath tore her new dress on the fallen limb of a tree, and blamed it all on Jimmy Woods who happened to step on the other end of the limb when it caught her dress, and they had such a quarrel that they went on the rest of the way in separate cars.

Eleanor Martin was especially unhappy, for in spite of her best laid plans her car was loaded up with two of the girls whom she detested, and the stupidest boys in the bunch. She would have protested, but by the time she reached the rendezvous, having had trouble with her make-up and been delayed longer than she realized, the others were all seated ready to start, and there was nothing to do but take those left standing on the sidewalk waiting for her.

One of the boys who had fallen to her lot was determined to drive the car for her, and after resisting as long as she thought she could she let him drive for a few miles, and during that episode they had two narrow escapes from a smash-up, and one pretty nasty puncture in the new tire which set them back several miles behind the rest of the party who went gaily on their way, shouting out that they would unpack and have the lunch ready when they got there.

Moreover Eleanor's conscience troubled her, for she knew her father would be cross about that puncture, and she knew she had broken her word to him in letting Fred Romayne drive.

Redmond Riley had brought a strange boy from New York with him, and this young man had a dashing way with him and carried in his hip pocket a flask which he kept passing around. Eleanor was too well brought up to partake of its contents, but she had not courage to prevent its being passed among the others in her car, and presently the whole carload became most uproarious, finally demanding to stop at a place on the way, where Red said they could get the flask filled up.

Eleanor knew that her father would not approve of such doings, and she had a few ideas herself of what was the correct thing to do; still she lacked moral courage to insist, and the consequence was that she suffered tortures all day both from her conscience which continued to annoy her, and also from the actions of the hilarious boys who were carrying things with a high hand. After the lunch eight of them jumped wildly into her car, which she had unfortunately left unlocked, and drove madly off through the woods singing and shouting at the top of their lungs, their feet scoring the new leather of the seat, their driver dashing along the wood's road without apparently noticing where he was steering, the brakes grinding in a loud scream just in time to save a collision with a large tree.

Eleanor ran after them shouting, pleading, wringing her hands, but too late. They dashed on and were gone for an hour and a half, returning with the beautiful new car splashed with mud and one fender bent. The stranger from New York had been driving. He had filled his flask again somewhere, and apparently had distributed it generously among the others, for they were all wilder than ever.

Eleanor had to lock the car and hide the key to prevent their going off again later, and in despair she climbed into the driver's seat and refused to leave it, saying she must drive the car herself or they could not ride with her.

She tried to get rid of Red and his friend from New York, but none of the girls wanted them, and the remainder of the day became a nightmare to her.

Moreover the moon which they had counted upon for their return drive, withdrew behind a cloud, and rain began to fall to add to their discomforts.

They arrived home long after midnight in the midst of one of the most terrific thunderstorms that the season had known, and those of the new dresses which had escaped thorn and briar, and crushing and wet moss and spilled cocoa, got a thorough drenching before their miserable young owners got safely into their respective homes.

Altogether Eleanor was not very happy when she met her father's stern eye and tried to explain why they hadn't come home at the time they had promised, and why the fender was bent, and the tire flat, and a long jagged scratch in the leather of the back seat. Tried also to explain the stain on the new carpet of the tonneau, and the strong smell of liquor that pervaded the whole dejected mud-splashed outfit.

Altogether Eleanor was anything but happy as she went to her room that night and she was not in a much better mood when she came downstairs the next morning so late that the breakfast table was cleared off and everything edible put away.

The Garner girls were not much happier either. They telephoned Eleanor that their father was very angry about the behavior of the crowd, for it appeared that some one had passed them earlier in the evening and recognized them, and had brought back a report of their doings which had spread through the town with various additions, and the Garner girls were in trouble. Their father considered them responsible to a certain extent. They intimated that he also considered that Eleanor had been responsible for the young men who were in her car. The whole thing was making a most unsavory stir, and the Garner girls were very unhappy.

Later there came word from Janet Chipley. Her mother was taking her away immediately. She did not wish her daughter's name to be mixed up in the affair. It appeared that Red and his New York friend had called upon Janet that morning to return a silver spoon which they had somehow carried away in one of their pockets, and had much offended Mrs. Chipley. Later advices from other members of the select junior crowd showed even more horrified parents as the day wore on and the stories grew. For be it known that the crowd that the Garner girls and Eleanor Martin belonged to had been considered beyond reproach, and now the young ladies sat in dust and ashes and indignity.

Euphemia Martin, as she resolved to try to have herself called hereafter, had spent a quiet evening in her room after her day's experiences, searching her Bible for the verse that Lawrence Earle had quoted. With the help of an old concordance from the library she found it at last and made sure that its words were thoroughly graven in her memory.

She went to sleep saying them over to herself, "Whatsoever things are true, whatsoever things are honest, whatsoever things are of good report; if there be any virtue, and if there be any praise, think on these things!"

And she had never in her life thought on any of those things. It had never made the slightest difference to her whether any one thought her true, or honest or of good report or lovely or anything else. She had gone on her own selfish way, doing what she pleased and boasting to herself that she did not care what people thought of her, feeling proud of the fact that she was going against public opinion. And here, it was in the Bible all the time that that was one of the things God wanted her to do, think about being lovely and true and having a good reputation.

Now she thought about it, there was another verse she had learned when she was a child, something about avoiding even the appearance of evil!

Well, it was strange that she should have run across this young man in this way. The very person she would have avoided if she had known he was there! And to think he should have been the one to show her the way in the darkness! Just that morning she had been wishing she had some one she dared ask what to do about making herself right, and then he had been sent! He must have been sent, for it was all so queer and out of the ordinary, everything that had happened the whole day! It must be God had sent him to help her!

She went over the story he had told her of his own awakening. That must be what old-fashioned people used to call "conversion." People didn't talk about such things nowadays, at least Euphemia had not heard them, unless it might have been a minister now and then mentioning it in a sermon. But Euphemia had never been in the habit of listening much to sermons.

But Lawrence Earle was sincere. She could see that. He believed everything he said and he carried conviction when he told about it. She felt sure he was right. She was comforted by the fact that God cared to guide her, and that He had promised to help her. She longed to know more about this mysterious life of the spirit that Lawrence Earle seemed to live in and understand. Could it be that a young, unloved, unlovely girl like herself could ever get that great hold on God that Lawrence Earle seemed to have?

And what a witness he was going to make for Christ! Why, he even cared to stop and witness to her, just a young, wild awkward girl with nothing about her to catch his interest.

Oh, what a great thing it would be to go about a living witness of Christ! For that one would not mind giving up anything else. But, of course she never could. A girl who wasn't considered good enough for the other girls of the neighborhood to associate with could never be fit for the indwelling of the great white Christ, the divine Savior of the world!

But perhaps He could make her fit! Lawrence Earle had said He was able to keep anybody from all kinds of falling, and to present them faultless—wasn't that the rest of that verse? They used it in benedictions. She knew it by heart because she had usually been so glad that the service was over that she followed the benediction to its end, ready to bounce out into the aisle the minute the amen had come. "Now unto Him that is able to keep you from falling, and to present you faultless before the presence of His glory with exceeding joy—" Did that mean that He was able to make one so faultless that it gave Him joy? He was not ashamed to present one whom He had made faultless, even before the presence of God's glory? How wonderful!

Euphemia had never thought about holy things like this before. But she lay for a long time in her bed in her dark room going over these thoughts, and at last she slipped from her bed to her knees and spoke aloud in a very low tone, as if she felt the Presence to whom she was speaking standing close beside her:

"Oh, Jesus Christ, if you are able to make anything out of me with my faults, won't you please take me, and do it? I don't see how you can, but I believe you can do it if you say so, and I do want to be faultless. I would like to be a witness for you if you think you ever could make me fit."

When the terrible thunder began to roll over the town, and the lightning flashes lit up the darkest corners of rooms, and the rain dashed in sheets against the windows, Euphemia lay sweetly sleeping on her pillow with a smile of trust on her young lips.

She came downstairs the next morning with a light of anticipation in her eyes. She was actually looking for God to answer her prayer.

Chapter Nine

THERE were two surprises in the Martin home that morning. The first occurred when Lawrence Earle drove up to the door in his car, and inquired of Johnnie whether his sister had recovered from yesterday, and if he might see her a moment. It is true that he spoke a name, one that sounded strangely to Johnnie—Euphemia—but he supposed Eleanor was meant, of course. Who but Eleanor was ever inquired for by a young man? Margaret the eldest sister, was married and in a far-away western home. Eleanor was the one to be called upon now. And naturally, Eleanor would be supposed to be recovering from her ride of the day before. Indeed, she had just arisen, and was taking a belated breakfast at that moment, by herself in the pantry. Johnnie, like the usual small boy, knew all his sister's comings and goings, and he was aware that this young man had been asked to join the ride the day before, also that Eleanor was much interested in him.

The living room was in charming order. This was owing to the careful thought which Effie had bestowed upon that clause, "whatsoever things are lovely" the night before. Effie began to see that there were a great many things which might be lovely, and that it was this clause in which she seemed to be most lacking.

Johnnie, having seated the guest, hastened to the kitchen in search of Eleanor.

"Say, Nell, where are you?" he called. "Come out o' there. There's a man in the sitting room to see you—that Earle fellow. He wants to know if you've recovered yet from your pleasure excursion, and I expect he wants you to go and ride; he's got his car, so you'd better get your toggery on. You look like a last week's milkshake in that rig."

Then Johnnie put his hands in his pockets and, having done his duty, whistled himself out of the kitchen door, before his sister had recovered from her astonishment enough to ask him any questions. She quickly laid down the piece of apple pie she was eating, and slipped up the back stairs to follow Johnnie's advice pondering the while why Lawrence Earle had come to see *her*, and planning what a delightful time she would have riding with him, the envy of all the other girls. She decided that he had probably come to make his excuses for not going with them yesterday. But why had he come to her instead of to those girls who had sent out the invitations? She was in a flutter of excitement, and tossed over her boxes and drawers for a certain string of beads she wanted to wear. Euphemia, in the next room, was getting the baby to sleep, and singing softly. The words floated through the half-open door occasionally; and down through the hall to the waiting visitor:

"I ask Thee for a thoughtful love,
    Through constant watching wise,
To meet the glad with joyful smiles
    And wipe the weeping eyes;
A heart at leisure from itself,
    To soothe and sympathize.

"I ask Thee for the daily strength,
    To none that ask denied,
A mind to blend with outward life,
    While keeping at Thy side;

Content to fill a little space,
   If Thou be glorified."

He smiled to himself as he listened and thought: "If that is Euphemia, and I think I know her voice, she did not need that I should guide her to Him, for she evidently knows Him already. Perhaps she has caught the secret."

Then Eleanor came down the stairs, smiling and fresh. Eleanor was very pretty, and she was graciousness itself now. She was pleased to have him call. It was kind of him and they had been so disappointed yesterday. Earle seemed a little surprised, but he was courteous. He asked about the ride and said it had been a perfect day, but other plans had prevented his going. He did not, as Eleanor expected, ask her to ride, though she was arrayed in the prettiest of garments. Instead after a few words about the weather, the roads and the town in general he told her she had changed a lot, that he shouldn't have known her, and then he asked if he might see her sister Euphemia. For a moment Eleanor was puzzled. She was just about to say she had no sister Euphemia, when it dawned upon her whom he meant, and she said, "Oh, Effie! Why, yes, I think the child is around somewhere. You never can tell where to find Effie. I'll go and see if she's been heard from lately," and she left the room bewildered. What in the world did he want with Effie? Had she been getting into some sort of a scrape and had he come to find out what she knew of it? Her face burned with shame over the thought.

Effie's low-voiced singing over the baby as she laid him carefully on Mother's bed in the darkened room, caught her sister's ear, and she hastened to summon her.

Effie had discovered that virtue brings its own reward to a certain degree, and was feeling real pleasure in the work she had accomplished, as she softly covered the baby with Mother's white shawl, and tiptoed out of the room. She was startled to find her sister Eleanor standing in the hall frowning at her. "For pity's sake, Effie!" was her greeting. "What a fright you are! Go and brush your hair and put on something decent. Lawrence Earle is downstairs and wants to see you. He wants to know 'if you have recovered from yesterday.' What in the world does he mean! Have you been getting into some scrape, and has he come here to let us know it; asking after you in a very polite way not to hurt our feelings? I just know you have."

But she found herself talking to the empty hall, for Effie, her face lighted up with pleasure that her new friend had come, flew down the stairs without waiting for brush or collar or any adornment, and never paused till she stood in the doorway, and realized her untidy working dress.

Eleanor, too vexed to know what to do, followed her sister downstairs, thinking to apologize for her carelessness, and find out, if possible, what was the matter. The busy mother passed through the hall at that moment, and they all met at the door just as Lawrence Earle was saying gaily:

"Good morning, Euphemia. How are you? Not all in after yesterday? Well you are some sport!"

Eleanor wondered with disgust if Lawrence Earle supposed Effie was one of the crowd, and had perhaps been the one to invite him yesterday. Likely he had gotten them confused, and she must set him straight at once before Effie got her head turned.

But the young man went on speaking:

"How about it? Do you feel like having a few minutes' exercise? I brought a baseball over. I'd like to see how my old pupil has progressed. Can you spare her, Mrs. Martin? Or is this a busy time, and should I wait till afternoon?"

"Why no, of course not, go ahead, dear," responded her mother, heartily glad that some real fun had come to her usually unwelcome daughter.

Effie flew upstairs to make a few changes in her apparel.

"You have a wonderful daughter!" said Lawrence Earle earnestly, looking from Mrs. Martin to Eleanor, "you certainly would have been proud of her yesterday. Not a girl in a thousand could have done what she did!" and then he turned as Euphemia, her eyes bright with pleasure, came flying back downstairs in a clean blouse which she had hastily donned "on the fly" as it were, and they went laughing off together into the yard.

"What does he mean, Mother?" asked Eleanor in an offended tone. "What on earth has Effie been doing now?"

"I'm sure I don't know," said her mother watching them with a half perplexed pleasure. "He isn't spoiled a bit is he? I was afraid he might have changed with all the adulation he has had."

"I'm sure I don't see how you can tell he isn't spoiled," said Eleanor discontentedly.

"I don't think he's very polite to say the least. He might have asked me to play too; I'm the oldest daughter."

"Great Cats!" said Johnnie who had come into the dining-room door and was listening. "Nell, you never could throw a ball, nor catch it neither. Wouldn't you make a great figure out there pitching ball!"

"Why, I thought you scorned ball-playing Eleanor," said her mother innocently surprised. "I don't suppose it occurred to him that you would care to play."

"Well, I wouldn't!" snapped Eleanor shortly. "I was only saying how impolite he was. The idea of his coming over here and making Effie a laughingstock in her own yard. I shouldn't think you'd allow it, Mother! I should think you'd put a stop to it before anybody sees her! I'm ashamed to have the girls know my sister acts that way."

"I don't see what you mean, Eleanor. Your sister is not behaving in any unseemly way, and as far as I can see she is very graceful in her movements. That little blouse she made out of your old white dress fits her very nicely."

"No, you never can see any harm in anything Effie does," said Eleanor. "You don't

126

care how much humiliation I have to bear on her account. That's nothing to you."

"Aw, shucks!" said Johnny watching out the window. "If you could sling a mean ball like that you'd be out there too, you know you would. You're just jealous, that's what you are, Nell!"

"Johnny! You mustn't speak that way to your sister!"

"Well! She is!" said Johnny vanishing out the back door to slump down in the grass by the edge of the ball space and watch the game, ready to run after the ball if it should elude the skilful catcher's hand.

Eleanor went discontentedly upstairs to watch the performance from her curtained window, but she managed to be sitting down on the porch when the two finally finished their play and came sauntering toward the house.

Mrs. Martin came through the hall with her arms full of clean laundry which she was about to carry upstairs as they came up the steps.

"I'll carry that for you, Mother," said Euphemia with new thoughtfulness, springing up the steps. "You don't mind if I go for a ride, do you?"

Eleanor made eager talk while the visitor

waited for her sister to come down, hoping that she would be asked to go along, and resolving to put Effie in her place if she did. The very idea of Effie's usurping the best new young man in town!

But Lawrernce Earle did not ask Eleanor to accompany them, though he was as pleasant as possible while he waited, and as he left he said to Mrs. Martin:

"You won't worry if I keep her out late this afternoon, will you? I've promised to show her a new road that she's never seen and Mother told me to bring her back with me to lunch. I think I demonstrated my ability to take care of her yesterday, didn't I?" and he touched his hat and went away laughing, as if they understood.

Euphemia's cheeks glowed as she looked back at her mother and sister, but she said nothing, and Mrs. Martin stood looking after them wondering.

"Something very nice must have happened yesterday, or something rather—" she paused for a word—"dangerous, perhaps." Her eyes took on an anxious look.

"Nonsense!" said Eleanor sharply. "Something disgraceful, I'll bet. That girl can stir up more trouble in a given time than anybody I know. I bet she just did this for spite, whatever it was, because she wasn't allowed to go on that picnic. I might have known, when she came around so softly sweet and asked Papa not to forbid my going, that she had something up her sleeve. I declare Mamma, I think it's terrible the way you let Effie disgrace us all!"

There were tears of vexation in Eleanor's eyes. She stood gloomily beside the window looking after them and drumming on the sill. "Mamma," she said as her mother passed again through the room. "Do you think it is quite safe to allow such a child as Effie to go off with strange young men? You know Lawrence Earle has been at college, and you never can tell how boys change when they go away from home."

The mother gave her a look of astonishment. "Why, Eleanor daughter, what can you be thinking of! Lawrence Earle is one of the finest young men I know. It seems to me you were very anxious but yesterday to go off with him yourself. I am afraid, if you would examine into your heart, you would really find something like jealousy there."

The mother passed on, and Eleanor went glumly upstairs to settle down to a novel.

She was presently roused, however, to answer the bell, and this time a handsome car driven by a liveried chauffeur was drawn up in front of the house and a gentleman, holding by the hand a lovely little child, entered and asked for Miss Euphemia Martin. He seemed much disappointed that she was not at home, and asked after her health most solicitously. Could he see her father or mother? When Mrs. Martin was summoned from the kitchen, accompanied by the ever-wakeful baby, he overwhelmed her with words of gratitude for her daughter's prompt and brave action, which had saved the life of his child. He was anxious to know if he had Euphemia's full name written correctly. He said the little boy had a small gift, a slight token of the gratitude they felt. He had telephoned into the city for it late the night before, and had it marked with the name the people who were standing about on the road had given him, so he hoped it was correct. The gift had come by special delivery that morning; and at a sign from his father the beautiful baby presented to the mother, a small white box, carefully wrapped and tied with white ribbon.

Mrs. Martin took the little white package and looked at it curiously, bewildered.

"But I don't understand," she said. "I don't know of anything that my daughter

Euphemia has done to merit any thanks. There must be some mistake. Perhaps it is another Miss Martin you mean."

"Oh, no," the gentleman said, "the grocer's boy directed me here. He said he knew the young lady quite well, and that she was very brave and fearless."

"But, what did she do?" asked the mother, fearful now lest this was another of poor Effie's escapades that would turn out to be not half so praiseworthy as the stranger seemed to think.

The caller proceeded to tell the story then to the wondering mother and sister, with all the details which he had gathered from the onlookers and Mrs. Martin's eyes grew bright with pleasure over the praise her little girl was getting.

"She was always quite fearless," said her mother. "I am glad it has served to some good purpose. I have sometimes despaired of her ever growing up and settling down. But I rejoice that my daughter was able to save this dear child's life," and she laid her hand tenderly on the little golden head of the boy who looked up at her with a confiding smile, and said:

"Hoss wunned an' wunned! I awful scared! Dirl 'top him. Nice dirl 'top horsey!"

When the callers finally left, promising to come again and thank the young lady personally, Eleanor stood watching them ride away with stormy eyes:

"Weren't there any men around to catch that horse without Effie having to rush forward and make a display of her riding? Effie is always putting herself forward. Here, let's see what she's got. Some worthless trinket I suppose. Such people think they can discharge a debt like that with a few words and a plaything," and with a most disagreeable expression on her face she reached out her hand to take the package her mother held.

"Eleanor!" said her mother sternly, "What can have come over you? I am thoroughly ashamed of your actions. You will most certainly not open your sister's package! It is hers to open when she comes"; and her mother left Eleanor feeling very uncomfortable.

Chapter Ten

OUT on the sunny road, under a clear blue sky, with a pleasant morning before her, rode Effie. At another time she might have stopped to think what the girls would say when they saw her companion, and she would have had a feeling of triumph. But her humiliation had been so recent, and this young man's coming had been so like an evangel to her, in her utter self-abasement, that she looked upon him with a sort of awe, and desired only that she might be worthy of this morning's great honor. So it was that she rode calmly by the Garners' place and never saw the two girls sitting on the wide front piazza, nor noticed Janet Chipley and Maud Bradley coming down the street, until her companion lifted his hat. She raised her eyes then, and when she saw who they were, the color flamed into her face. Lawrence Earle noticed it, but gave no sign. He had had a purpose in directing their course around that way. A young cousin of his, quite an intimate of the little Chipley sister and the little Garner sister, had unfolded some of her beliefs regarding Effie Martin to him at dinner the night before, when he had told his mother of his afternoon's experience and the young girl's part in it.

"Cousin Lawrence," she had said earnestly, "I think those girls treat Effie Martin real mean. They wouldn't let her go with them yesterday. I heard them talking. They say she climbs trees and bites her nails and isn't old enough. But I 'most know she wanted to go real bad. Don't you think they were mean? They wanted you though, real much. I heard them say you would be the lion of the 'casion."

He had laughed at the little maid's earnestness, but some inkling of Effie's feelings and what she had been through began to dawn upon him, and his indignation grew toward those other girls, who he felt needed a lesson. Therefore he rode with Effie through the main part of the town. But out upon the smooth country road, two good miles between themselves and all disagreeable circumstances or memories, he made her forget herself, and think only of the beauties about her. He even quoted one or two rare bits of poetry, in order to watch her face and see if their beauty touched her soul and awakened an answering chord; and he enjoyed her wonder and evident delight in all he said. He also discovered that she had been no mean reader herself, for a girl who made no pretension to things literary.

They had a most delightful morning. Euphemia felt that she never had enjoyed herself so much before. It was on her way back that she summoned courage to ask a question. "Would you mind telling me just what you meant yesterday by repeating that verse? How could I make my name fit? I hunted out the verse last night, but I'm not sure I understand."

"Certainly," said he, his face lighting up at her question. "Suppose we stop under this tree and you can read the verse for yourself in the original. I always carry my little Greek Testament with me in my pocket."

"Oh, but I can't read Greek, you know."

"Perhaps not, but I think you can read your own name. It is in that verse. Do you know that it is there in the form you wear it in your name? 'Whatsoever things are lovely, whatsoever things are εὐφήμια,' those are the exact words."

They stopped under a chestnut tree, and the young man took out of his pocket a copy of the New Testament in Greek that looked as if it had seen much use. He opened to chapter and verse as if he knew the way to it well, and pointed out the words to her reading slowly until she recognized her own name in the queer Greek characters.

"You see," he said looking at her eagerly, "all the things which go to make up a good report are summed up here: to be true; to be honest; to be just; to be pure; to be lovely. If we are all these we are sure to have a pretty good report given of us. But the trouble is, most of us are not all, nor even many of these things all the time, and we find it quite impossible of ourselves to be either, so what are we to do? The Book says, 'think on these things.' You know one's character generally takes color from what one thinks about most. If I think about and love the world, I am worldly. If I think about evil I make it easy for evil to develop in me. Now if you think much on these things which are Christly, they are likely to grow in you, so that you literally become εὐφημιά , of good report. But that is not all. Did you notice the last clause in the next verse? 'And the God of peace shall be with you.' So you see you don't have to do it alone. It would be utterly impossible to grow Christly by our own efforts. It is really Christ who works it in us. Christ dwelling in us. And when you begin to 'think on these things' you open your heart for the Christ to come in and dwell there. And He has promised to keep your heart in all peace."

It was all new to Euphemia. She listened with her soul in her eyes, and afterward she could shut her eyes and seem to remember every inflection, every flash of his eyes, and every curve of his lips as he spoke the words that seemed to mean so much to himself. He seemed so eager to impart his own knowledge to her.

All too soon the morning was gone, and they drove back to the Earle house for lunch, and now indeed Euphemia had a taste of unsought triumph. For the Garner girls and Maud Bradley and Janet Chipley came driving past just as Lawrence Earle turned into his own driveway, and they all saw that the despised Effie Martin was with him, and that they were laughing and talking as if they had been having a good time together. And he was taking her home to lunch! That was plain to be seen, for Mrs. Earle was even then on the piazza, waiting to receive her guest. The traffic lights held the girls until they had seen Mrs. Earle come forward and greet Effie affectionately, as if she quite expected her, and was pleased at her coming.

"Did you ever!" said Janet Chipley crossly. "Well, he always was queer! So that's that! Effie Martin of all girls! But of course he doesn't know what she is!"

"Oh, he'll find out soon enough," proph-

137

esied Ethel Garner. "Effie Martin can't keep herself in the background long."

But what they did not know was that Effie Martin was gone, and there was to be in her place Euphemia Martin, a different girl, as different as if she had indeed been born again.

The beautiful day was over at last, and Lawrence drove her home leaving her at her father's door with the promise of coming for her soon again.

Effie came slowly into the house thinking of all the happy, helpful day, and wondering how she should begin to live her new lesson, when she was met by Johnnie, bursting at every pore with information and curiosity.

"I say, Eff, hustle along there, won't you? There's a package here for you, and Ma wouldn't let us open it till you came. A fellow in a big swell car and a pretty little boy that looked like a girl was here and left it for you. Say, I think you were real mean not to say a word about that runaway. You must have had a regular picnic of a time."

She opened the little white box wonderingly, and found inside another white box of velvet lined with blue, and in this lovely case a tiny platinum wrist watch set about with jewels, tiny diamonds and sapphires, and on the back of it was inscribed: "To Euphemia Martin, in grateful acknowledgment of her brave action in saving the life of Clinton Carroll."

She looked long at the dainty, jewelled time-piece and the inscription. Here was a testimony to at least one good action she had done. This "Euphemia" inscribed on the precious metal surely meant "of good report." She looked at it so long and so thoughtfully that the others, who were impatient to see it, pressed closer and took it from her, and as they handed it from one to another exclaimed over its beauty and the bounty of the giver and what the younger ones termed "Eff's luck." She slipped out from among them, leaving it still in their hands, and stood looking out of the window deeply stirred. What a lovely thing had come to her as a sort of seal and memorial of the new life she was going to try to live. She was roused from her thoughts by her sister Eleanor's words:

"The idea of giving a child like you such a magnificient jewelled watch! It will never be of the least use in the world to you. It's too fine for you to wear. Where would you ever go, to dress up enough for that? And when would you ever get the silks and velvets fine enough to wear with it? You'll just have to consider it a medal of good behavior. Perhaps by and by, when he moves away and forgets about it, you might sell it and get something worth while."

"Humph!" said Johnnie, looking at her curiously; "I bet you'd wear it quick enough wherever you went if you got it. You'd never think anything too fine for you. Gee whizz! a thing like that's fine enough without any silks and velvets. I think I see you swelling round with it on! You better put it away carefully, Eff, or you'll find it 'out for the evening' some of these fine times when Nell goes to a party."

He was interrupted in this speech by a stinging slap on his cheek, followed by a box on his ears, and Eleanor blazed angrily at him for an impudent little boy. In the midst of this, Effie took her beautiful watch and fled to her room. She had been very happy but a moment before, but now her happiness was clouded. She had seen like a flash, since she turned from the window at her sister's words, two distinct ways in which she might work out that "whatsoever things are lovely," and she did not want to work them out. She sat down in her little rocker by the window to think, and look at the beautiful watch. That seemed to embody to her the first thing. She had seen that Eleanor liked the watch and would enjoy it very much if it were hers. Of course she could not give it away when the gentleman had given it to her. That would not seem right, but she might lend it to her sister sometimes. That seemed a hard thing indeed to her. Her pride and her love of possession and carefulness for her watch all clamored together in her against such a proceeding. Why was it necessary? Eleanor had a watch of her own for which she had saved the money from the small handfuls that fell to her share. She never would allow Effie to wear it. In fact, Eleanor had never shown any great amount of love for Effie; why should she put herself out for her? Ah "whatsoever things are lovely"! If she would win love, she must be lovely. It would be lovely to give Eleanor this pleasure sometime.

She put her watch away with a sigh at last, wondering if she ever could come to that sacrifice, and resolving to think it out and try to do what was right. There was yet another subject to hold her thoughts—her brother Johnnie. Could she help him in any way? He and she had always been more nearly like companions than she and Eleanor, in spite of the difference in their ages. She knew that she had some influence over Johnnie. Perhaps she could win him to be a better boy. Then she thought of the words Lawrence Earle had spoken that morning about God being with you, "the God of peace," and she remembered how many times she had heard people talk about having "the peace which passeth understanding." How she wished she had it! How glad she would be to know and feel that the God of peace was beside her, and that she might look up to Him as she had done to the young man and ask Him to show her where to go and what to do! He would love her. She felt sure He would. Perhaps it was true that He was beside her now, and this throb of something strange like a new joy was His smile as He told her He was glad she wanted His love.

In a sort of shamefaced way she went and locked her door, drew down the window-shades, knelt beside her bed and prayed. She was not used to praying, except at night when she went to bed, and then only as a sort of form which she had kept up since babyhood. She was not quite sure that she had really prayed when she rose from her knees, uncertain whether she really ought to add an amen to such an intangible prayer as that, but in her heart she felt that in that act of kneeling and praying she had taken the decisive step toward beginning a new life. She had meant by it to let God know that she was intending to "think on these things," and wanted Him to come and be with her and show her how, and most of all, to love her. She drew up her shade and looked out of the window through the green branches of the trees to the exquisite blue of the sky and said softly to herself: "I almost believe that I love God a little, and I wonder why, because I know I did not feel so yesterday, nor last night. I wonder what has made the difference? It seems as though He has sent me some kind of a message that made me know He was here." She closed her eyes a moment just to be glad in the thought. It was so new to her to stop and think at all, or to have any one's love around her in that way. Then with her characteristic quickness, she began to look around for something to do. "I must go down at once and begin," she told herself, smiling. And a careful observer would have seen in that smile, a touch of the peace which was to settle down upon her brow, more and more, as the days went by, and she went on "thinking on these things."

She opened her bureau drawer for one more peep at the lovely jewelled thing that seemed to be so much alive with its musical little tick going, going on all the time—her very own. And yet even in the few minutes since she laid it there, and although she prized it just as highly, it did not seem to her a selfish image of her own pleasure, but rather a token that she was beginning a different life with more joy in it. The watch might be used in God's service now without causing so severe a pang as a few minutes before.

Chapter Eleven

WHEN Euphemia opened her door she heard a sudden piercing scream from the baby downstairs somewhere, and her feet fairly flew to see what was the matter. Was this an opportunity to carry out her new resolves?

As she opened the dining room door a strange scene met her eyes. The baby was seated on the floor with something in his hands which he seemed to be fighting, while he screamed at the top of his lungs and appeared to be in mortal terror.

The cat was rolled in paper from which she was unable to free herself, and was rattling frantically about the room, now landing on the top of the sewing machine and entangling herself further in a spool of silk, now arriving on the dining table which was already set for the evening meal.

Johnny from the porch doorway was howling with joy, and Eleanor was laughing with all her might. Neither of them had made the slightest attempt to rescue either baby or cat. The kitchen door opened and Mrs. Martin appeared, a kettle of hot potatoes in one hand, the colander in the other, saying in an anxious voice: "What is the matter? Why don't you do something, some of you?"

A quick investigation showed that both cat and baby had become entangled in the sheets of fly paper which the careless servant had left on a chair when she started to set the table for dinner. In such catastrophes it was the custom in the Martin family for the children to stand by and enjoy the discomfiture of the victim until their mother came to set things right. They were running true to form this time, and so great was the power of habit that Euphemia on first sight had almost joined them in their merriment. But a glance at her mother's face, reminded her of her vision of better things which she had just had upstairs during her few moments of communion with her unseen Guide. Instantly she knew that here was her chance to begin her new life.

√ "Johnny, catch that cat!" she cried, springing to rescue the frightened baby who had just started to apply his face to the flypaper. "Never mind, Mother, we'll have it all right in a minute," she called, and then she rapidly pulled the paper from baby while she held his fat, flying little fists firmly and directed Johnnie, who had proceeded to have a regular game of catch with poor pussy, to the great danger of everything breakable in the room.

The cat was frightened almost out of her nine lives. She flew from one article of furniture to another, and came within a hair's breadth of knocking over the milk pitcher and carrying the butter plate to the floor with her.

"Open the door, Johnnie," called Effie, "and get me some water and a rag, quick.

Maybe this stuff is poisonous and the baby has some of it in his mouth."

Eleanor was aroused to help then, and they finally managed, after trying water and soap and kerosene, to get the sticky paper from the poor, pink fingers of the frightened baby. Then Effie took him, and they went to look for the cat and Johnny; and by and by kitty and baby were comfortably clean and baby was hushed to sleep. Effie felt very hot and tired for the baby was heavy and his struggles had made him hard to hold. She looked dubiously down at her new brown suit, and found several daubs of fly-paper varnish on it, and knew that it would take a vigorous cleaning to make it as good as new again. The new life wasn't going to be all rose-color after all she perceived.

Then it was dinner time, and she went in to be greeted by her father with an unusual smile. "Well! so it seems our girl was very brave yesterday," he said. "They tell me, Mother, that she hung on to that horse after it had reared and lifted her from the ground three times. There were plenty of men about, but none of them moved to help. Our little girl did it all. It is terrible that you went through all that, Daughter, but it was a very brave thing to do. I am proud of you! It was a great thing to be able to save a life!"

Euphemia's cheeks grew red with the unwonted praise and she caught her breath. So much virtue and so much praise coming to her all at once! Even more than she deserved.

"If there be any virtue, and if there be any praise" chanted a little line in her soul, and then added, "whatsoever things are honest."

A sudden chill came over her gladness. Ought she to tell her father that the account he had heard had been overdrawn? It was so sweet to hear his praise! And, of course the details did not really matter. Still, "Whatsoever things are honest." Suddenly she looked up:

"I didn't stop the horse quite alone, Father," she said with a clear-eyed look. "Lawrence Earle came almost immediately and put his hands over mine and held him or he would have got away from me. He was a very strong horse. But all I did was catch him first when there was no one else near enough to reach him. I was on my wheel, you know."

"Oh, indeed!" said Eleanor sarcastically. "I thought they were making a terrible fuss over a little thing. I think Lawrence Earle ought to have that watch, then, instead of you."

"Nevertheless, it was a very brave thing to do, Daughter, and you deserve all the praise any one can give you," said Mr. Martin. Then turning to his elder daughter he said severely, "Eleanor, it seems to me that it ill becomes you to make remarks like that. It was Lawrence Earle himself who told me the story of the rescue. He was driving his car and was practically helpless at the critical moment. He had to stop his car and spring out, but he said that before he reached your sister's side, the horse had reared three times, lifting her from her feet, and that it is a miracle that she was not killed! Your criticisms are in very bad taste. You ought to be rejoicing that your sister is still alive."

Euphemia was deeply grateful to her father, and her heart throbbed with a new love for him, but her sister's scorn stung deep in the midst of her joy. It was a little thing perhaps, but it hurt. Johnny had been watching her thoughtfully, and after dinner he said to Euphemia:

"Aw gee! Eff, whaddya go an tell that ya didn't do it all, for? Nell has to get her old

149

face in everywhere. I wouldn't a given her the chance."

"But Johnnie, it wouldn't have been honest," said his sister.

Johnnie gave her a quick look. "What's the difference?" said he.

"It makes a difference, Johnnie," she said with a sigh, thinking of all the difference she wished it would make in her.

"How long since?" he asked curiously.

"Johnnie, I'm going to try to be honest always after this. Why don't you, too?" She said it earnestly, almost wistfully, and the boy, quick to follow a leader, and interested always to do something in partnership with some one older than himself, assented.

"All right, I will." He evidently had no question of what would and would not be honest. He surveyed his whole life in one comprehensive glance, and knew in a general way wherein he would have to make a change. "And say," he added, "do you mean we'll size up together say every Sunday night, how we've done it?"

Effie foresaw trials in this proposed plan but she also saw possibilities, and she agreed. Then she went in to see what her new Guide had for her, of work, or trials, or thought.

The next day looked bright ahead of her

as she went to bed that night after a last look at the dear little jewelled watch lying in its satin bed.

But she certainly would have been astonished if she could have heard what her sister Eleanor was saying at that very minute when she laid her head upon her pillow.

Eleanor was spending the evening with the Garner girls, and they were out on the porch talking over their unfortunate picnic.

"What do you think," Eleanor was saying. "My sister Euphemia—"

"Your sister *who?*" screamed Janet Chipley. "I never heard you call her that."

"Well, we do, a great deal," said Eleanor. "Mother feels she is getting too old for Effie now. But what do you think? She had the velvet after all yesterday. She didn't get to go with us, but she had the guest of honor all to herself, and an adventure besides. I suppose you'll hear about it to-morrow for it will likely be out in the paper so I may as well tell you. Euphemia is very shy about mentioning it. She never said a word herself till Lawrence Earle came over and spoke about it. He and Euphemia are awfully old friends, you know. He used to pet her a lot when she was nothing but a baby. He really is responsible for my sister's boyishness. He taught her to pitch ball, you know, when she was quite little."

The girls were all agog, listening with bated breath and jealousy in their eyes. Had they not seen the hated Effie riding with the much coveted prize of the town? What did it all mean? And Eleanor talking in that half proud pleased way about her sister! Oh, if Euphemia on the way to dreamland could just have heard and seen! But perhaps her guardian angel knew it was best not, and so drew a kindly veil for the present, and sheltered her from too much uplifting praise.

But it is a pity that Johnny too should have been asleep, and not have been there, for Eleanor's good, at least.

For Eleanor was enjoying not a little reflected glory from her sister's brave deed. She sat back in the big porch rocker and swayed back and forth with satisfaction.

"Yes indeed!" she went on, "they've always been quite chummy. I suppose if we had asked my sister there wouldn't have been any doubt but that she could have coaxed Lawrence to come with us. Strange I had forgotten how fond he was of her."

"But you know Effie,—I mean Euphemia,—hasn't the slightest idea of being set up about it all——"

152

"But what did she do?" interrupted Maud Bradley jealously. "You're not telling us."

"Do?" said Eleanor smiling, "oh, nothing, only chased a runaway horse that was about to dash over the quarry ledge out by Brocton's Corner, and saved the life of Charles Clinton Carroll's only son and heir! Wasn't that some trifle? And she nearly got killed herself incidentally. Dad and Mother are terribly upset about it. They can hardly speak about it. And Effie,—I mean Euphemia—comes in as casually as possible and never tells a word!"

She waited a second for the impression to deepen, and then she went on:

"It seems Lawrence had seen the runaway himself and had been chasing them, only of course he was hampered by his car, but he got there as quickly as he could—the horse was terribly frightened by the sound of the car coming after him, and all the people standing round were simply petrified with fright. And Effie—Euphemia—would certainly have been killed if Lawrence hadn't arrived in the nick of time and just barely saved her. She was a couple of hours coming to, and Lawrence brought her home of course. Oh, yes, she's all right this morning, went out and played ball with Lawrence for a while and then went off to lunch with him and his mother. Of course they begged me to go but I simply couldn't think of leaving Mother with all there was to do this morning, and anyhow it wasn't fair to Ef— Euphemia!"

Eleanor was making quite a case of reflected virtue, and rather enjoying it. She studied the faces of her friends, and saw a wave of incredulous perplexity passing over their faces. It was time to change the interest:

"But you ought to have seen that darling baby, little Clinton, when he came with his father to thank Eh—phemia! His mother couldn't come, she was so overcome with the shock, so Mr. Carroll himself came and he couldn't say enough about E—phemia, how wonderful and brave she had been. It seems the horse lifted her clear off the ground three times trying to shake her when he reared. It must have been frightful! It seems as if I couldn't get it out of my mind. I couldn't sleep a wink last night for thinking about it!"

Amazement held the tongues of her companions silent. This was an entirely new Eleanor! Was she real?

"Mrs. Carroll is coming to-morrow to

thank Ef—phemia! But they sent the darlingest gift! I simply had to go out of the house not to open it when it came, Ef—she wasn't at home you know—but of course I wouldn't have opened it for the world till she came. That is half the fun in getting a present, to open it. Don't you think so? Well, when she got home we all stood around and watched her, and what do you think it was? Why the darlingest platinum watch, all jewelled! It's perfectly precious! Wait till you see it. Ef—she would have let me wear it over to-night to show you if I had asked her, but I couldn't bring myself to,—not the first night. But you'll see it. It is the sweetest thing I've ever seen. I'm so happy for her I don't know how to stand it. Isn't it great? And it has a perfectly stunning tribute to Ef—her bravery engraved on the back. It will be something she can keep forever, and hand down to her children. We're all so pleased for her. It's better than getting something yourself to have a thing like that happen to your sister, you know."

And all the girls sat in wonder, and Oh-ed and Ah-ed, and decided that after all they ought to have asked Effie Martin to their picnic. How perfectly humiliating to have been left out of all that!

Chapter Twelve

Euphemia arose the next morning with a heart full of joyful anticipation. She seemed to be standing on the top of the world looking over into morning land. What was it that made life so well worth living? Ah, she was a new creature with a new name, and a new Friend to help her. Two new friends in fact. One the God of peace who was able to keep her from falling and to present her faultless before God's glory, His pure white searching glory! The other the friend who had led her to that God of peace and made her understand that He was her Savior, able to save her at every turn of the way.

She wondered shyly whether she was to see her friend Lawrence Earle again soon. Of course she couldn't expect that his interest in her would keep up. He was four or five years older than she was, belonged in a different social set from any she would enter if she ever did belong to any social set; she doubted it. Also, he had many vital interests. Among other things that they had talked about he had told her of his hopes to go and witness for God in some corner of the earth where witnessing was most needed. He had told her he was studying, preparing for his life's work, and she knew he expected to be very busy that summer, attending conferences here and there where notable Bible teachers were to be present. She sighed wistfully and wished that she might be able to hear some of the good things that he was to have, but perhaps he would come over now and then and tell her about them, and her heart thrilled at the thought of how she would get books and study by herself, so that she would be better able to understand what he told her when he did come.

Then she went downstairs to eat her breakfast and help wash the dishes, for it was the maid's day off; and almost as soon as they were done he appeared in an old sweater with his baseball in his hand.

"I thought we might have a little practice this morning," he said smiling, and she went joyously out to play, feeling that life had never, never had so much joy for her as it did just now.

They played for an hour,—and the Garner girls had collected quite a little group of the girls behind the hedge and were watching, though of this Euphemia was scarcely aware, she was having such a good time. And then they sat down under the cherry tree with the sunshine glinting between the branches on their heads, while Lawrence read to her a chapter in his new Testament in Greek and translated as he went, demonstrating a new thought that he had found.

It seemed like heaven opening to the girl whose inner life had been starved so long, and the thought of the summer stretched wide and sweet and helpful as she sat with dreamy eyes and listened to words which opened up a new life to her.

It is strange how lives touch for a moment in this world, and then move apart for years. How interesting it will be hereafter, if we are allowed to study the wise workings of Providence, and understand all the whys and wherefores!

It would seem to a casual observer that Euphemia Martin needed that sweet new influence that had come into her strong young life and turned it into a new channel, needed it for some time to come, in order that she might be strengthened and taught, and not fall back. But perhaps the Father saw otherwise, saw that this was a soul that could be put to the testing almost at once.

However that was, right there in the middle of a sentence of Gospel truth Johnny came rushing into the picture with a message from Mrs. Earle. A telegram had come that her sister in California was very ill, dying perhaps, and wanted her to come. Would Lawrence come home at once?

Of course Lawrence would come at once. He sprang up startled, and turned for an instant to the dismayed girl who stood up beside him, her eyes full of disappointment.

"I'm sorry, little pal," he said, using the old name he used to call in her baby days when he taught her to throw a ball. "I've got to go—probably will have to go with Mother. If I don't get back you'll know. It's been awfully good to have these nice times with you. And I won't forget—! You won't forget Euphemia! You'll go on thinking of these things, won't you?"

Euphemia, with a sudden choke in her throat, and a sudden stinging of tears in her eyes, put her hand in his and promised. She would go on. She would not forget!

"And we will both pray—!" he added, "for—each other!" Then with a quick pressure of her hand, and a sudden lighting of his eyes that she never forgot, he was gone.

And that was the last time that Euphemia Martin saw him for five years!

They left on the noon train for California. Of course Lawrence went with his mother.

He wrote Euphemia a beautiful letter en route explaining and saying how sorry he was that they could have no more games or rides, or reads together, but promised to send her a book he thought she would enjoy which would help along the lines they had been interested in.

And so Euphemia Martin entered into her testing time.

It would seem that the Devil might have been laughing in his sleeve at how quickly the props were knocked out from under this girl's new resolves. Now, now how would she be able to live her saintly life of virtue without any one to show her the way? The old life, the old temptations, the old hindrances, the old jealousies all were left, and it would be easy to drop back into the old ways again.

And for a little while it seemed to the girl that this must be inevitable as her dream of the summer joys faded, and she knew she must struggle on her new way alone.

Yet she was not alone. She remembered that she had "the God of peace" with her and He was "able and willing to keep her from falling," any kind of falling her new friend had said. If she would only let Him!

Well, she would let Him as far as she knew how!

It cannot be denied that she felt disheartened, when she found that her new friend had gone away. It could scarcely be called a disappointment, because his friendship had been so unexpected; but his help had been so great that for a few days, she was utterly discouraged, and made so many failures and relaxed into her old ways so frequently that she seemed, even to herself, to merit most of the sharp criticisms she had heard of herself. But her soul had grown sensitive by the little praise she had received, and she dreaded again to deserve cold looks, and the kind of despairing reproach her mother had in her eyes sometimes. She wanted her mother's approval, and she wanted most of all to be true to her name. Why was it that she failed so miserably? "The God of peace shall be with you," the promise read. Why did He not help then? Perhaps it was be-

161

cause she did not ask Him aright. Perhaps if He was with her she ought to talk with Him more. In a general way she knew that people who were trying to be Christians read the Bible and prayed every day. She had never stopped to ask herself if she were a Christian before, but now that she thought of it, she supposed she was. But she realized in her heart that she was a very poor specimen.

She was standing by the window one night looking out into the dark. There were no stars shining. Her lamp was still unlighted. All her life looked dark to her. She felt herself very wicked. The tears chased one another rapidly down her face. Her thoughts grew bitterer until sobs came, and sometimes grew audible as she sank down upon her knees beside the window, and abandoned herself to thinking how utterly hateful everything was, including herself.

Mrs. Martin, passing through the hall on the way from tucking up the baby, heard a queer little wail coming from this daughter's room and went to investigate. And Effie, crying too hard now to notice the opening door, felt her mother's work-hardened hand in gentle touch upon her head, and then her mother's arms around her tenderly, and her mother's voice said: "My poor Euphemia,

162

what is the matter? Will you not tell Mother all about it?"

For a few minutes the girl cried all the harder, just because of the sympathy and love that had come to meet the ache for it in her heart. But by and by the sobs ceased, and she sat up and told all, beginning with that afternoon under the trees when she had heard herself talked about, every little word she could remember, even down to the biting of her poor finger nails.

It was very hard for her mother to feel that her girl had been so talked about, and thought of, by others. And perhaps it was a hundredfold harder, because the mother could see at once that it was because of habits formed in her as a child, which should have been broken; because of the lack of gentleness and politeness, and sweet womanliness that she should have tried to train daily in the growing soul. Mrs. Martin blamed herself for not seeing this before, and guarding her daughter. She blamed herself none the less that her life was already so overcrowded, and she so overburdened, that there seemed not one minute of time left for anything more. She sighed heavily, and was indignant with those girls, and yet could not altogether blame them. But oh, she did so want all her children to be good and beloved and admired! Effie went on to tell of her ride and the runaway, and then her meeting with Lawrence Earle, her talk with him and his helpfulness. And the mother blessed him in her heart.

Mrs. Martin had never talked her religion to her children. She had not known how to open the subject with them; but she did trust in her Lord, and she lived her life with gentleness and patience, even through days that were hard and wearing to her soul. And now that Effie brought her story to her mother, that mother knew how to point her on the right way she had chosen, and to give her much-needed encouragement. Well for her that she had a parent who was acquainted with the Lord Jesus Christ. Before Mrs. Martin left her daughter that night, she came back from the door hesitating and gently, quickly, drew her down beside her on her knees. Then in a low, almost inaudible voice, that trembled with the fright of hearing itself in prayer before another, she asked her Heavenly Father to guide her little girl. She kissed her and was gone. It had been very hard for the mother to pray aloud, because she had never been accustomed to such a thing. She had been embarrassed even in the dark. But she had done it.

After that night her mother never called her anything but her full name, Euphemia, and then she began to teach the baby to call her so, and by and by Johnnie and her father and the others took it up, and within a year she was known to them always as Euphemia. The mother hoped by this constantly to remind her daughter of the meaning of her name, and she did not hope in vain. Euphemia was glad to lose her old and rather despised name and gain a new one with her new life.

There began days in which the mother said gently, "Euphemia, I would like you to help in this," or "Euphemia, if you want to be helpful this morning, there is that," or "Daughter, dear, that disorderly room is a burden to me this morning. Could you set it to rights?"

This helped Euphemia. She always remembered what she was trying to do when her mother spoke like that. There followed too, many evening talks with Mother, brief necessarily, because of the many cares, but helpful. It was Mother who suggested ways of helping Johnnie, and who seconded her efforts to please her elder sister, and Mother who bade her not despair when she had failed and forgotten all her good resolves. And it was Mother who arranged it so that she should have a certain little quiet time to herself in her room undisturbed, to "think on these things," and to pray. This, after all, was the source and centre of her life. She learned to commune with Jesus in those daily thinking times.

And the wonderful peace of God "which passeth all understanding" began to settle down upon her brow in unmistakably sweet and gentle lines. The others could not help but feel it. She was careful for others; careful of their feelings, and of her own actions, to make them pleasant to others. She curbed her desires more often now and tried to do as others wished and not as she would please.

Not that she accomplished this all at once. She had days when everything seemed to settle back to something worse than it had been at first, and when she seemed to lie again upon that green moss and hear those voices on the other side of that hedge criticising her. At such times she would sometimes be brought back from almost despair of heart by glancing down at her hands. The nails upon her fingers were now well-shaped and carefully cared for, with dainty white rims, and the pink flush of health. There was no need for her to hide those hands now. She never bit her nails any more; neither did she fidget in church. Certainly, in those things she had been helped by hearing what others thought of her, though it had been very bitter at the time, and well-nigh destroyed her faith in life and humanity.

Lawrence Earle did not return to his home town within a few weeks as he had told Euphemia he would, and as he had confidently expected to do when he left. His aunt lingered at the point of death all through the summer, and finally crept slowly, but surely back to life. She seemed to need her sister, and Mrs. Earle did not feel that she could possibly leave her, and as there was nothing especially urgent to call Lawrence back alone he remained.

He wrote Euphemia that he had found a wonderful Bible school out there where he was taking a course that was most helpful, and from time to time there came to her pamphlets and books, and a little magazine which both cheered and helped her on the way in which she had set her course. It put her into touch with a new world, a world of the spirit, where she found that they were a great fellowship who believed this way, and were waiting upon the Lord and "thinking on these things." When she first realized this she felt greatly strengthened, and it seemed easier to know there was a host of people scattered everywhere doing what she was trying to do.

Then there came a letter one day from Lawrence Earle telling her that he had received a call to go out to India to do some "witnessing" for a year or two, and had decided to accept it. He was sorry not to get back for another game of ball, and another chance to read Greek with her, but it could not be helped, and he felt sure this call was from God. He sent by the same mail some more literature and a precious copy of a remarkable translation of the New Testament directly from the original which he said would help her greatly. In the package was also a small but beautifully bound copy of the Scofield Bible which he said was a gift from his mother to her. His mother and aunt were planning to take a trip abroad and would accompany him part way, as his aunt was able to travel.

So that was that, and Euphemia looked up from her letter with a sad but patient face. Well, she had known in her heart that she would probably never see him again, when he went away, but it was somehow a wrench to be sure that he would not be back for a long time, if indeed he ever came. India! It seemed like going out of the universe! A kind of blankness filled her soul. But then she realized that she must not feel that way. She must be thankful all her life that his way had touched hers for a few days, for oh, what a difference he had made in everything to her! She could never lose the help he had given her, even though she never saw or heard from him again.

So the days and the weeks went by, and an occasional post card with strange pictures and stranger post mark reached her. Once or twice a brief letter came telling of the wonders of the new land but they were hurried letters from a busy man. Already he seemed like a prophet who had larger interests than just to help her little life.

Euphemia put the letters all away in a little old writing desk with inlaid top and a lock and key, which had been the property of her Aunt Euphemia long years ago, and had fallen to her lot. Nobody would ever open this, and here she hoarded all her little treasures. Sometimes she took them out and read them over, for they seemed somehow related to her Bible closely, and always there were quotations and suggestions which made her Bible study more interesting.

But the days grew into months, and the months into two and then three years and Lawrence Earle was still in strange lands, connected with some island mission, preaching, teaching, travelling and establishing new stations, training new teachers. He did not write much about himself when he wrote at all. She gleaned most of her information concerning his movements from the little magazine which came to her regularly from its far home, and gave her a vivid picture of life as he was living it.

Still, it all seemed quite far away and unreal, and more and more she came to depend on her Bible and prayer for her daily strength.

Euphemia had finished school, had graduated from high school with honors not a few, in a gown that was faultless as to fit and appointments, and amid open admiration from her classmates. For the years had brought her a measure of good looks all her own, and her new ways had taught her to be always well groomed, and she looked as pretty as any of them. Flora Garner, who had been ill and had to stay back a year, was graduated in the same class with her, and seemed quite willing to be friendly with her, always making a point of walking to and from school in her company, and Euphemia was not any more the lonely wild thing she used to be.

But Euphemia had worked hard, and had not taken much time for social life aside from keeping up her tennis, swimming and skating, and these latter she managed to do very often in company with her brother John, who with a group of his "gang" as he called them was devoted to her and always ready to have her join them in their sports. So, in a measure, she was the same independent girl, walking much apart from the girls of her age.

Her mother worried over it sometimes, but she had her hands so full with Eleanor's affairs that she had little time to do anything about her next daughter's social life. The father said: "Well, Mother, don't worry, perhaps it's a good thing for the child. She hasn't half as many temptations as Eleanor, and she has twice as much character as all those silly girls put together."

"But she'll grow old all alone," mourned the mother, "and perhaps she'll blame us."

"Not she," said her father. "She's too sweet a nature for that. And she'll not grow old alone, don't you be afraid. Somebody 'll snap her up some day, somebody that knows a good thing, and then what'll we do without her? Besides, if she should happen to grow old all alone as you say, she'll be such a blessing as she goes that her life will be a happy one anyway. So don't you worry about Euphemia! I have always told you she would turn out all right. You do your worrying for Eleanor! She needs it! Euphemia doesn't."

And Euphemia, who happened to be in the library at the time consulting the dictionary, heard them talking, and smiled tenderly. At least she had won the good report with her father and her mother.

And Euphemia had developed a beauty of a kind, also.

Perhaps it was the peace which sat like a light upon her sweet face that made people turn when she went by and say:

"Look! Did you see what a distinguished-looking girl that was?"

Her soft olive complextion, untouched by cosmetics, still had the healthy wild-rose glow, and her dark eyes had lost their unhappy restlessness and wore a constant light of settled joy and peace in them. Her heavy hair she had not kept bobbed, but had it grow, and it set off her vivid face softly, in rich dark waves that would not brush entirely smooth, and needed no curling iron or any such thing, for it had a permanent wave of its own. Neither did she need lipstick on her lips, for they were red with nature's own touch.

Neither was her body big and awkward any more, for her outdoor life, and her suppleness had made the muscles firm and given a fine slender line to her erect carriage. Altogether she was good to look upon, and Eleanor often watched her half jealously because of her free graceful movements so utterly without self-consciousness.

For Eleanor was having a time of her own, and while she was a little more tolerant toward her sister now, because Euphemia often did a great deal for her in the way of mending and making over her desses, and relieving her of her natural share of the household labors, still she had very little time or thought or love for anybody in the world but Eleanor Martin.

Chapter Thirteen

ELEANOR was going to be married.

Sometimes it seemed to Euphemia as if Eleanor felt that no one worth-while had ever been married before. Eleanor was determined to have the very best of everything, and plenty of it.

Euphemia overheard her father telling her mother that things at the office were in a very bad mix-up and money was going to be scarce for the next six months, and he wished she would go as easy as possible in spending for a while. But Eleanor wept bitterly when Mrs. Martin suggested buying more inexpensive clothes than she had picked out, and the household resolved itself into a gloomy place. Then up rose Euphemia.

"Eleanor, why can't I make your lingerie? I'm sure I could save a lot of money on it. It is ridiculous for you to pay five and six dollars apiece for those little wisps of crêpe de Chine and lace when we could make them for a dollar or two apiece."

"The idea!" sneered Eleanor, and dissolved into tears once more, "If—I ca-can't have a decent outfit, I w-won't get m-m-married at all."

"But you don't want Father to go into debt for it do you? He can't buy things without money, can he?"

"He can borrow some money!" said Eleanor sharply from behind her sopping handkerchief.

"Well, Mother says he can't. Mother says he has already borrowed up to his limit to save the business from going to the wall. Now it seems as if it was up to us to do a little something to help. Father went without a new suit when he bought the car to please you. He went without heavy underwear and got pneumonia the winter he bought your new piano. He goes without things all the time to get us the necessities of life. I know for I heard him talking to Mother. And there are going to be enough new things you'll have to have for very decency without spending a fortune on imported underwear. I'm going to make some for you."

"But you couldn't *possibly* make them the way I want them. Those imported things have lines, and nobody but a French dressmaker can get those lines. Besides, they are perfectly darling, with little lace insets and rosettes, and satin rosebuds. It would be perfectly dreadful to have just plain things in my trousseau. I would be ashamed to show them to the girls!"

"Well, I don't see that it would be an absolute necessity to show them to the girls, but even if it was, I don't see that this has any point. You can't buy what you can't afford, and if you spend all that money on under things you can't even have a wedding dress, let alone hat and shoes and going-away things. I heard Father say the check he gave you was positively all he could spare and we must make it do."

"Well, if this is your wedding go ahead and do what you like. Make your old patched-up lingerie. I won't wear it."

"You'll have to, if there isn't any other. And Eleanor, you can take me down to the stores and show me just what it is you would like to buy, and if I can't make exactly as good and pretty and everything for less than half the price I'll say no more. I can copy anything I ever saw in that line."

It ended in a compromise. Eleanor and Euphemia went shopping, saw all the prettiest lingerie, and Eleanor purchased a single garment of each style she desired for a copy. So Euphemia laid aside the precious books and her own preparations for her coming winter at college, and plunged into the intricacies of glove silk and filet lace, and lingerie ribbons, pink and blue and apricot and orchid, until the whole upper story of the house looked like a rainbow.

There were endless discussions in which Eleanor was constantly either weeping angry tears or blaming her parents for the things they had not done for her, until life became almost intolerable.

Mrs. Martin went about with a constant sigh on her lips, and her brows lifted in the middle anxiously. Sometimes Euphemia noticed that her lips were trembling and her hand trembled as she raised it to her aching head. And Euphemia was the buffer between the two. Euphemia gave up her own ways and her own plans, and took as much of the burden as possible from her mother's shoulders.

In those days also Father Martin was grave and abstracted, coming late to his meals and hurrying away having eaten scarcely a bite sometimes. He lived on strong coffee. Euphemia, as she went about trying to help, trying to lift the burdens her parents were carrying, trying to hide Eleanor's selfishness, and to lessen the household expenses, and to fling herself generally into the breach, wondered what the end was to be.

Then it developed that the wedding dress must have some real lace on it, and Eleanor demanded the best. Thirty dollars a yard was the lowest price she would hear to, and said with a toss of her head that even that was not nearly as good as Margaret had had on her dress.

Now Euphemia had in her precious inlaid box, wrapped in soft old tissue paper, several yards of wonderful lace, yellow with age, her heritage that came with her name, Euphemia, handed down from Aunt Euphemia, who had come into possession of it through her husband's family. It was lace such as Eleanor never could hope to own, and Euphemia knew that she had often envied her for having it. And of course the sacrifice that presented itself to this patient thoughtful younger sister was that she ought to lend her lace to her sister. It was much the same breath-taking sacrifice that she had once contemplated about her watch, only that sacrifice had never been permitted by her parents. When she had hesitantly proffered the watch once to Eleanor to wear until her own was mended, her father had most summarily given his command:

"That is Euphemia's watch, and it is a valuable thing that she will want to keep always. She alone is responsible for it, and it is not right for any one else to have it. Eleanor, you get along without a watch until your own is mended. You are too careless to have charge of Euphemia's, and we can't run any risks of losing a thing like that. It couldn't be replaced, you know."

Euphemia stood at her bedroom window in the starlight when the idea first came to her that she must lend Eleanor her lace for the wedding, and had it out with her soul. She felt a little dismayed that she found so much selfishness still lingered in herself, but resolved that it should be conquered, so after kneeling down to ask for strength to make this sacrifice as if it were a joy, she sought her sister's room at once, not wishing to leave the matter until morning lest she might weaken.

She found her mother sitting in the moonlight beside Eleanor's bed, trying to reason with the weeping Eleanor.

"Listen, dear," Euphemia broke in, with a throb of almost joy in her voice, "Don't worry another minute about that lace. You're going to wear mine, of course. You know every bride has to wear something borrowed,

'Something old and something new,
Something borrowed and something
    blue,' "

she chanted gaily. Switching on the electric light she took out the lace in all its filmy yellowed richness. It settled down upon the pillow in a most amazing heap, a treasure that a princess might have been proud to wear.

"Oh, my dear!" said her mother with a mingling of relief and protest in her voice. "Your lace! Your wonderful wedding lace! The lace that Aunt Euphemia left you!"

Eleanor sat up and mopped her red eyes and stared.

"You're not going to let me wear your lace, are you Pheem?" she asked in astonishment. "You certainly are a peach! Say, Pheem, you won't mind if I don't tell it's yours, will you? You don't mind if I say it's an heirloom?"

"But it was to have been *your* wedding

lace, my dear," protested her mother fearfully, seeing in Eleanor's request a hidden danger.

"I'm not being married myself yet. The lace won't wear out in one wedding by any means," said Euphemia lightly, trying to put down the rising lump of apprehension in her throat.

"Oh, Mother, Pheem's not the marrying kind, and anyhow she doesn't care for dresses. She's too good!" declared Eleanor cheerfully, slipping out of the bed and going to the mirror to drape the rich flounce of lace around her shoulders, and tip her head to one side to get the effect. "It suits me, doesn't it? It's just perfect. Pheem, you're a peach! Would you mind if I cut it, darling? There's enough to make a flounce on the skirt too. Isn't it gorgeous?"

"No!" said Euphemia sharply wheeling toward her lace. "No, I *cannot* have it cut! I'll arrange it so it will be pretty without that, but it must not be cut. It's an heirloom!"

She turned appealing eyes to her mother, and Mrs. Martin seconded her.

"Certainly not, Eleanor, you mustn't think of cutting the lace. Isn't it enough that your sister has loaned it to you without your suggesting such a thing? It would be a defamation."

Eleanor pouted.

"Oh, dear! It wouldn't hurt it in the least. It could be pieced together again without any trouble. Well, I don't know as it will do then! I'll have to buy some after all! I couldn't think of putting it on if it doesn't look right."

"It isn't in the least necessary to cut it, Eleanor," said Euphemia patiently, and she took pins and tried to show her sister what effect could be got without cutting the lace.

Eleanor haughty, offended, and only half convinced, finally yielded to the inevitable, knowing in her heart that no money she could ever get together could buy half such priceless lace as this.

It was like this all the way through. Eleanor wanted a caterer, and Mrs. Martin insisted that they could not afford it. She and Euphemia baked and planned, and worked with might and main as the day drew near. And then it appeared that there was a bridesmaids' dinner to be planned for, and that she must furnish the bridesmaids' dresses; or at least Eleanor had told the girls she was going to do so in order that they might be just what she wanted. She had planned for eight bridesmaids, and she insisted that Euphemia should have a new outfit of most expensive materials. And there were gifts to the bridesmaids, little gold vanity cases. Eleanor went to the city herself and got them, and had them charged to her father at a most expensive place where he had never had a charge account before. He was vexed almost beyond endurance.

All these things were accomplished finally as Eleanor desired, in very self-protection for the family, for Eleanor wept and wailed her way through till she got what she wanted, silk and satin and lace, flowers and ribbon and frills.

"Vanity of vanities all is vanity," quoted Euphemia as she surveyed the house two nights before the wedding. "And what is going to happen after it is all over?"

Eleanor was marrying a man from another State, and a number of his relatives came to the wedding. Eleanor demanded that a good many of them be entertained at the house. There seemed to be no end to the things that Eleanor wanted. Would it ever be over, Euphemia wearily wondered, as she toiled down to the laundry and ironed a couple more old curtains for a window that had been forgotten in a room that had been hastily requisitioned for an extra guest room. Wearily she dragged herself up the stairs again and found a rod and a hammer and screws and put up the curtains. She looked in on the array of handsome presents set out on their white-draped tables in the upstairs sitting room.

"Whatsoever things are lovely!" she quoted to herself, and wondered if things like these counted in the scheme of life. Of course they did count, somehow, else God would not have made so many lovely things, but hadn't they somehow got out of proportion, sort of overrated their value? Weren't there other things that were lovelier, and more lasting? Euphemia was too tired to philosophize about it.

She saw her mother dragging up the stairs just then, looking old and tired to death, and forgetting her own weariness she flew down, and gathering her little mother in her strong arms she carried her up and put her down on her bed.

"Now Mother dear!" she said stooping to kiss the tired brow, "you're not to get up until early morning. No,"—as her mother tried to rise, "I don't care how many things you have left undone, you are not to stir until morning. Wedding or no wedding, guests or no guests, you have got to rest."

She helped her mother undress in spite of protests, and put her inside the sheets, turned down the light and closed the door. Fifteen minutes later the bride burst into the house and stirred them all up again. She woke her mother from the exhausted sleep into which she had sunk at once, with the startling announcement that Everett's great uncle (Everett was the name of the bridegroom) was stopping off on his way to California and wanted to meet her parents and see the presents. No, he couldn't stay overnight. He had to catch the midnight express to meet an appointment, but he was bringing a set of solid silver salts and peppers, and her mother simply must get up and meet him.

Euphemia protested, and even tried to frighten her sister by saying that their mother would not be able to go to the wedding if she did not get some rest. But Eleanor swept her aside and dashed into her mother's room, switching on both lights and deluging her startled mother with the whole story in a breath.

"You must put on your violet silk, Mother. He won't be here to the wedding and he won't know it is *the* dress. I want you to appear at your best. I'll get my curling iron and fix your hair. You'll have to hurry like the dickens. Everett only got the telegram ten minutes ago. He's driven right down to meet him, and the train is due in about five minutes. Everett is *very* particular about him. He wanted me to make you understand that. He is *very* rich, you know."

Half bewildered, and sodden with weariness Mrs. Martin dragged herself up and let them dress her.

Euphemia with set lips went about getting her things and putting up her hair, while Eleanor sat down and hurried them like a bumblebee.

When the car drove up their mother lay back in the big chair in the living room looking white and spent in her pretty new dress. Euphemia was so worried about her and so angry at her sister for being so inconsiderate that she very nearly said some sharp things to Eleanor. Eleanor acted almost as if it didn't matter at all whether or not there was any mother left after the wedding was over.

But Eleanor would not have heard even if she had said the words that sprang to her lips. She was fluttering to the door to meet the guest.

And after all the great uncle was deaf and indifferent and nearsighted and didn't even seem to see their mother, merely acknowledging the introduction haughtily, and passing on to the room where the presents were spread out.

Euphemia hurried her mother back to bed as soon as they were gone, thankful that Eleanor had gone down to the midnight train with them to see the disagreeable uncle off again.

Euphemia, the next night, in her golden draperies, her arms full of yellow expensive roses, walking slowly, steadily, up the church aisle as maid of honor, studied the stolid flabby face of the bridegroom and wondered what Eleanor saw in him to make her willing to sacrifice her whole family to please his dictatorial fancy. If Everett wanted to do expensive things for Eleanor after she was married, that was all right, but he had no right to insist on Eleanor's family mortgaging their very souls to make his wedding appear great before his friends and family.

Coolly she walked up the aisle, her regal head lifted, her face full of a something that seemed to lift her above the rest of the procession and make people look at her, rather than watch for the bride. "Just look at Euphemia," they whispered. "Isn't she beautiful! She's prettier than her sister."

But Euphemia was looking her future brother-in-law over and weighing him in the balance as it were, in the light of his actions during the past weeks, and she was sorry for her sister. That selfish little puckered mouth, those expressionless eyes set too close together, the characterless chin. Wherein had been his power over Eleanor? Was it his reputed wealth? She almost shivered at the thought as she drew nearer to the waiting bridegroom, and dropped her eyes to her flowers, taking her place at one side to await the bride. A wave of thankfulness went over her that it was not herself who was being married to Everett Wilcox. Would Eleanor be happy? Oh, would she? She had never been happy at home, although she had always got almost everything she cried for. But if one might judge from that stubborn, selfish mouth Everett would never be one to give in to weeping. Poor Eleanor. For after all, disagreeable as she had been, Eleanor was her sister and she loved her.

As the awesome words of the marriage ceremony went forward Euphemia's thoughts followed them tremulously. Such terrible things to promise, if one were not *sure*. How could Eleanor promise all those things for Everett? Her very soul revolted at the thought. She felt sure that she herself would never be married. There would never be any one who would care for her who would be wise enough and great enough and dear enough to give one's self to in such solemn pledges.

She came out from the ceremony with a saddened heart. It seemed as if they had just handed Eleanor over to suffer somehow. She could not get away from the thought. Strange that this feeling should have come down upon her so suddenly. Perhaps it was because she had been too busy before to realize that her sister was going out from the household forever.

It was over at last, the showers of rose leaves and rice, the white ribbons on the car, and the shouts and shrieks as the couple made their way to escape. The last guest was gone at last, the last hired servant paid, and the door locked. Euphemia turned to see her little frail mother sink suddenly down in her silken garments, a small, pathetic heap of orchid silk with a white, white face above it.

She cried out as she sprang to kneel by her side, and her father rushed to them, and knelt on the other side, his face ashen-gray in the garish light of the rooms still decorated for the wedding with flowers he could ill afford.

They got her to bed and telephoned for the doctor, but it was almost morning before they settled down to get any rest themselves. Even then they hardly dared to sleep, for their hearts were so anxious.

The next morning Mrs. Martin tried to get up, but found she could not. She said she was only tired, and would get up in a little while, but when the doctor came in a little later he wore an anxious look and asked a great many questions, and commanded that she lie still for several days.

The several days stretched into a week, and then two, and three, and still she was unable to get up and go about.

At first the doctor talked cheerfully enough saying she needed a good long rest, but as the weeks went by it became evident that the trouble was more deep-seated than they expected. The poor nerves which had stretched and stretched until they almost snapped did not react, and Euphemia and her father gradually began to realize that the mother who had carried all their burdens and smoothed all their ways was down and out, and it was a serious question whether she would recover at all.

The knowledge of it came upon Euphemia like a crushing blow after the long hard going, for there was the house to be kept, and the poor servant utterly unable to cope with the situation, to say nothing of the mending and cleaning and baking, and the four-year-old baby to look after every hour in the day. There was her mother to be cared for like a baby herself; and there must be the most tender care, or she might slip away from them in a breath.

Mrs. Martin seemed satisfied only when Euphemia was with her. Of course a trained nurse might have relieved the situation greatly, but there was Mr. Martin harassed with a business crisis, submerged in debt, and struggling to pay some of the enormous bills that Eleanor had contracted for the wedding. The plain fact was they could not afford a nurse. And there was John, older of course a little, but still full of noise and mischief, and seemingly eager to coast down every wrong pathway of life that presented itself to his willing feet. More than half of their mother's burden had been this same John, whose companions and habits had been for two years past wholly unsatisfactory and the last few months a plain daily anxiety. Something must be done for John. There was no end. And nobody but herself to fill the breach and bear all the burden. And there were her beloved books, and her dreams of college by and by, and a wider sphere, although there was no need to complain of the narrowness of her sphere just now. It seemed to embrace almost every class and variety of work.

She sat in her room and thought about it awhile after the doctor had gone, when her mother and the restless four year-old were asleep. "Whatsoever things are true, whatsoever things are lovely, if there be any virtue, and if there be any praise," kept going over and over in her mind. She was accustomed by this time to putting all her actions to that Philippian test. She knelt to pray and rose to shut her hopes and her books away in her closet, and turn the key. Then she went down to her daily duties. This time she did not find the cat and the baby in the fly paper, but she found dismay and dreariness, for mother was upstairs sick, shut away from household troubles. Mother could not bind up a cut finger, nor kiss a bumped head, nor get a boy bread and jelly when he was hungry, and the worst of it all was that there was uncertainty how long this terrible state of things might last. The young hearts whose heaven was Mother's face could not see any light.

Then Euphemia found that she could comfort; she could think to do this thing and plan for that thing, and give up her own ways and plans; teach a spelling lesson to one, tell a story to another, and yet with the help of God keep patient and sweet through it all.

She still kept her little time by herself alone to commune with Jesus, or she could not have done it. Here she brought all her troubles and worries to think about. Sometimes it seemed so strange to her to think her life, that had always somehow been under a sort of cloud, was cut off from things that other girls had. She would go back in her memory often to that lovely day and that ride when she met Lawrence Earle and recall the only really grown-up pleasure she had ever had in all her young womanhood and wonder if it would always be the only one. Very likely it would, because she was growing old so fast. Poor child! She felt almost gray-haired.

But she did not sigh after those things long. Perhaps it would have been harder for her if she had been accustomed to going out a great deal. She was so continually busy and so really interested in her daily round that she had no time to be sad-hearted now. She sometimes got out her books too, for after the first few months of self-abnegation she saw that it was not necessary for her to sacrifice all her reading and study, and so she was not growing stupid. Sometimes when all was quiet and dark she would wonder to herself if the only person besides her mother who had ever promised to pray for her had forgotten. Probably he had long long ago forgotten her existence. It was a year since she had received even a post card from him. She was not even sure in what land he was at present exiled. If he thought of her at all he probably remembered her only as a disagreeable little girl whom he had tried to help to peace and happiness. And how wonderfully he had done it! If his witnessing in foreign lands for the rest of his life brought no results, he yet might count a humble star in his crown for the light he had brought into her discontented young heart. She would bless him always for it.

And what would she have done under this crisis if she had not found a refuge and stronghold in Christ? Surely the prayers of Lawrence Earle had been what had kept her from slipping away from God during those first months when she had been so discouraged, and perhaps they were helping even now. It gave her comfort to think that this was so and to feel that somewhere, somehow, she had an earthly friend, as well as a heavenly, who would at least care, and pray for her, if he knew her need. Then she would drop softly asleep and waken to another day full of labor and sunshine, for she was the sunshine of her mother's room.

Chapter Fourteen

MRS. MARTIN went down to the verge of the grave and lingered for weeks, merging into months, but at last, slowly gradually, so gradually that they could hardly be sure from day to day whether it was true or not, she began to creep back to them again—to take a little interest in their coming back and forth to her room, tiptoeing in with bated breath to watch her quiet face upon the pillow, to open her eyes and smile, to lift her hand one morning for a flower that Euphemia brought in, and then to ask after the baby, and want to see him.

Eleanor had not come home. They had

not told her how ill her mother was. The doctor said it would not do for her to have the excitement of Eleanor's coming.

Eleanor was "doing" the West in a wildly exciting wedding trip with all the accessories that money could provide. She wrote brief, breezy, occasional postals home, saying very little and conveying less. Euphemia seemed to feel an undertone of discontent even yet, and wondered, but there was little time to think of Eleanor.

Her mother was coming back to them, from the grave, and Euphemia's heart was gay with deep sweet joy. God had heard her prayer. Almost with awe she gave thanks. It seemed that she had come very close to Christ during her time of trial, and was coming to trust Him more and more restfully.

The day that her mother was first able to sit up for a little while was like a grand holiday. Father came home and sat with her, and brought roses! The kind he used to bring mother when he was courting her! And Euphemia noticed with another thrill of joy that the worn look was passing from his face, and his tired eyes were lit with new hope.

"Well," he said after he had sat for a

while holding his wife's hand, and looking at her hungrily. "Mother, I guess it won't do you any harm to know we're going to pull through in the business now."

"Really?" said Euphemia springing softly up and coming to lay her hand on her father's shoulder.

"Yes, we signed the big contract to-day. We get it all, and it means that by this time next year we'll be entirely out of the hole. We are practically now, only the money won't all come in at once. But we're standing on firm ground at last, thank God. And Euphemia, little daughter," he added, turning to the girl, "it's partly due to you. There was a time just after Mother took sick when I thought I couldn't weather it. And then you took hold and lifted burden after burden from my shoulders, and you stayed at home from college, and saved all that expense, and cut down the expenses here at home, and saved Mother for me. Little girl, I never can tell you what you have been to me, to your mother, to John and to the baby and all of us! You are a daughter such as no father and mother ever had before. Isn't she, Mother?"

And the mother's eyes lighted with the old sweet light as she said tenderly:

"She's all that and more."

Euphemia thought that her cup of joy was filled, but her father went on:

"There's another thing, Daughter, too, that I must mention while I am singing your praises. I want Mother to know what you have done for John. Mother knows how anxious we were about him. He had got going with a bad crowd and it seemed as if nothing could stop him, but somehow you have woven an influence about him that has pulled him away from it all. He came down to the office to-day and told me he wanted me take him in and train him for a partnership. He wanted to begin at the bottom and go up as fast as he was able. And I told him I'd be glad to. It will be better for him than fooling his time away at college the way he did last year. And I think he really means business. I'd have been glad to have him have the rest of his college course, but he says, and I agree with him, tht he can go and take the rest of his course later if he finds he needs it. It is never too late to study. And he knows I cannot afford to send him just now. He says when he goes he's going on his own money. And I feel that that is the right spirit. But I think his change of attitude is all due to his sister!"

It was sweet living those days, with Mother coming back fast to daily life now, and the spring coming on, and all the good things her father had said to think about, and Euphemia went about with a continual smile upon her lips.

And then, one day when Euphemia was walking home from an errand with her hands full of lilacs that a neighbor had sent to her mother she noticed that the windows of the Earle house were open at last, and a few minutes later met another neighbor who told her that Mrs. Earle was returning that afternoon.

Euphemia came home with her eyes bright with the news. She wondered to herself many things. Would Lawrence Earle come too? Probably not. She knew that his mother had been during the past year in California again with her invalid sister, and that the sister was not expected to live long. That was the news that had drifted back to the home town. In a general way Lawrence Earle was supposed still to be in foreign lands pursuing an occupation which the town was beginning to call by the name of "missionary"; some queer new kind of missionary, they said he was, doing something about Bible teaching.

Mrs. Earle had indeed returned, and began at once to set her house in order, and it began to be rumored that her son was coming later and would perhaps spend the whole summer with her. The story drifted out and around without Mrs. Earle's having even dropped a hint of any such thing. But some of her neighbors gathered, perhaps from things she had not said, that her son was going to bring some one home with him, presumably his bride. The suppositions grew to the proportions of confident statement, and were spread abroad as such. They came to Euphemia Martin's ears. Now Euphemia Martin was too happy over her mother's recovery to be other than glad over anything, and when she thought about this report at all, she wondered if Lawrence Earle's wife would be one in whom she could confide. Of course she would, she told herself, for he would choose no other than a good and true and lovely woman. And so in her heart she liked to think the coming Mrs. Earle would be a friend of hers. She held Lawrence Earle in a kind of awe, as some one higher than the ordinary mortal who had condescended for a little time to help her. He had forgotten her long ago, but she would always revere him. Euphemia would always be of humble mind after that severe experience she had had of seeing herself as others saw her.

One bright spring morning, when Mrs. Martin was feeling quite well and was able to be about the house once more, doing what little her efficient daughter had left for her to do of household tasks, Euphemia picked a great bunch of fragrant violets from the bank in their back yard, and with heart throbbing over her temerity and cheeks flushed slightly from the excitement of what she was about to do, went timidly to call on Mrs. Earle and leave her gift of violets.

She had a pleasant call. It seemed delightful to her. Mrs. Earle put her arms about her, drew her gently in, and called her "my dear." It all seemed very, very charming. Euphemia wished she had ventured before, and was even moved to ask some of the questions that in times past had troubled her so much and which on account of her mother's illness she had been obliged to solve without a counsellor. Before she went home Mrs. Earle showed her some photographs of her son, and several pictures taken during their trips abroad. In two or three of them there were other friends, whom Mrs. Earle said had been travelling with them. One sweet-faced girl was among those. Euphemia wondered if that was the coming Mrs. Earle, Jr., but lacked the courage to ask. She carried the vision of that face home with her and began to make a friend of it at once. Mrs. Earle asked her to come again, and there was begun a friendship which to both became very pleasant. Thus the springtime passed and summer was already at hand, and scarcely a day went by but Mrs. Earle ran over to bring some delicacy to her old friend Mrs. Martin, or Euphemia ran in to take some message from her mother. The old friendship was renewed, and knit the closer between the two older women, because the young girl was dear to them both.

And nearer and nearer drew the day for the homecoming of the son, but Euphemia somehow was strangely silent when the mother spoke of him. It seemed a subject in which she now had no part save as an onlooker. A glad one, of course, but still a mere outsider.

Chapter Fifteen

LAWRENCE EARLE boarded the New York Express, and after settling himself comfortably, took an unopened letter from his pocket. It was from his mother and had arrived just as he was leaving for the station. Being attended by a friend with whom he had spent the night in New York, he had put the letter by until he was at leisure on the train. He leaned back to enjoy it. His mother's letters were always a luxury. He read on through page after page of the closely written letter, smiling here and there at some sentence or expression which sounded so like his mother. He was greatly amused at the story she had to tell him of his supposed marriage, and stopped in his reading several times to look out of the window and laugh heartily. His mother had much talent in describing the words and tones of some of her many curious neighbors, and her son enjoyed her bits of quaint humor.

"They've settled it all, my son, even down to the bride, and whether she is to have charge of the house or not. I don't know what they will say when you come home without her. And I must say, my boy, though I know I should lose much of your precious society and be no longer first in your thoughts as I have been, that I could wish it were true, for you know, I cannot always stay with you, and you are getting to be 'quite a man.' "

At that sentence the young man smiled while yet the moisture gathered in his eyes, and a tender expression about his mouth.

The quotation was from the oft-spoken comment of an old neighbor who used to annoy him when he was a child by always telling him that he was getting to be "quite a man." When his mother wanted to be playful she often used the phrase. There followed some words about a certain young woman they had met abroad, and he stopped his reading once more to look thoughtfully out of the window. But at last he seemed to shake his head slightly and went back seriously to his letter. There was a description of the changes she had made in certain rooms, and of repairs and additions she thought it would be pleasant to make. There were little items of pleasantry about the town and the people. She told of the changes in certain families during their absence. "But there is no one who has changed more and for the better than your little friend, you will remember her, Euphemia Martin. She called to see me soon after my return in the spring. She seems to be a very lovable girl. I hear good things of her on every side. She has not only beauty, but character in her face, and not only that, but chastened, sweetened character. She is one of Christ's own children. I liked her sweet and gentle manners and her neat and graceful dress. She certainly has grown into a lovely girl, and is going to be another such as her mother was before her. Her mother was a beautiful woman before she took upon her heavier cares than she was able to bear. She, by the way, has been very ill for the past two years, and Euphemia has become the mainstay of the home, and the very life of her mother. I am really growing extravagantly fond of her. I had no idea she would ever develop into such a lovely character. Some power must have changed her, mightily, for I remember people used not to like her, and now every one in town has a good word for her. The pretty sister, Eleanor, whom I always thought looked selfish, you remember, has married and gone to California to live, and to tell you the truth I am thankful for I was always afraid you would become fond of her. You thought so much of the older sister Margaret when you were a mere boy. But Eleanor was no more like Margaret than night is like day. Euphemia seems to be more like Margaret, yet with an added charm which I cannot quite describe. You will have to see her to understand."

The letter went on to mention other friends or neighbors.

"Maud Bradley married a movie actor and there are rumors that she is very unhappy and thinking of applying for a divorce. Ethel Garner and her sister Flora are both married and gone, Ethel to New England, Flora to live in the south, Virginia, I think. Janet Chipley was killed in an automobile accident. Her little sister Bessie, you remember, with whom you used to play tennis, has grown into a pert little upstart of the modern times, with her hair cut close like a boy, and an impudent loaferish way of intruding herself into the public eye. She is very pretty, but exceedingly unpleasant to watch. She seems to have lost all sense of all the graces of womanhood.

"Do you remember a flashy little girl with copper-colored hair who used to wear bright yellow and burnt orange so much? Her name was Cornelia Gilson. She married your friend John Babcock. I think they ran away and got married, and John's father was so upset by the affair that he had a stroke of paralysis, and has never been able to get around since. I understand that Cornelia is making

John very unhappy. John looks twenty years older than when you saw him last. His hair is beginning to turn gray. He will be glad to see you again. He looks so wistful I feel sorry for him. I thought you ought to understand the situation before you see him. What a pity he could not have married some one like Euphemia Martin instead of that worthless, heartless little flirt!"

There was more in the same strain about other friends and neighbors, and a page telling how happy she was to have her son coming home at last to stay in his own country, and how delighted she was that he was to be employed in the Lord's service in a great work that was opening up.

When Lawrence Earle had finished reading he folded the letter thoughtfully and put it into his pocket.

All the time he had been reading he had been conscious of a pair of scrutinizing eyes turned upon him by a grizzled old man who sat across the aisle. He had been so occupied that he did not look at the man until the letter was folded and put back in his pocket, and then he became aware of that steady gaze once more, and instantly recognized an old farmer from near his native town. Lawrence Earle, as a little boy, had many a time hitched his sled to this man's load of wood. He rose and went to him at once, and the man seemed pleased beyond measure.

"Wal, yas," he said, "I am a good piece out o' my way. Been up to Bawston to my brother's funeral. I calc'lated to git back yesterday, but couldn't settle up things in time. I be'n a-settin' here spec'latin' on whether this was you or not. You seem to have growed some, and yit you ain't changed so much, after all."

The old man eyed the clean-shaven tanned face before him with keen satisfaction. There was something about Lawrence Earle that was most winning. The old man was tremendously flattered that he had come over to speak to him, and that he had remembered who he was. There were not so many young men in these days who bothered to talk to plain old men. But Lawrence Earle always was somehow different from other boys. The old man grew talkative, giving bits of information about the changes in the home town; how the courthouse had been torn down at last and a new one built, how the Presbyterian church had a new tower for the chimes that Mr. Blakesley had given in memory of his wife; how they were building two new public schools to accommodate the children; how the old political boss was dead and the new one had no use for farmers and was doing all he could against the farm bills they were trying to get through.

Then he relapsed into gossip about the townspeople:

"And there is that youngest Martin gal; they used to call her Effie. There ain't anybody more changed than she. She's growed up strong and straight as a young saplin', and she ain't lost none of her sooppleness either; she can pitch a baseball as good as ever. I seen her do it last week at the church picnic. She's just as fine, an' purty and healthy-lookin' as ever, spite of having nursed her mother through a long sickness for nigh about three years, and took care of the house and her father and all. She'd be a fine wife for some young feller. Why, sir, that gal was jes' the mainstay o' that family. Her pa, he couldn't akep' up nohow, with his wife down with nervous prostration for two year goin' on three, if that gal hedn't a done fer him and cheered him up. They do say she's done ez well ez her mother could by them boys too, and her a little slip of a thing that hed never done a thing but play, when her mother was too sick."

The young man went back to his seat after a time, and mused on what he had heard. So the little girl had been thinking on those things of good report, all these years, and had found the virtue, and the praise.

At New York he changed for his homeward-bound train, and here again he met a friend, a clerk in the home bank, on his way back from business in New York. They talked together a few moments, while they waited for the train to be called. "Speaking of changes," said young Brownleigh, "do you remember a little Martin girl, a regular tomboy? Effie, they called her. Well, sir, you wouldn't know that girl now. She dresses plain, but awfully neat and well-fitting, and they say she makes all her own clothes too. Oh, yes, she's good too, altogether too good for comfort! But a fellow would almost be willing to be good to get a girl like that to smile on him."

Lawrence Earle listened in wonder, and a growing delight. How strange it was that he should begin to hear Euphemia's praises sounded the moment he came near the home town!

And then, at the station he was met by an eager group of very young girls, headed by his own little cousin, among them the Bessie Chipley of whom his mother had written. There was a small Garner girl, and a small Bradley sister and a number of other children who were mere tots when he went away. They surrounded him noisily and demanded that he make a "date" with them at once before any of the older girls had a chance to invite him. They considered that he was their own property, their friend of the years. One would have thought to hear them talk that he was to have nothing else to do but attend parties and rides. They talked eagerly, and all at once. He felt that same note of hardness in their speech that his mother had deplored. Yet they were still children. Perhaps they could be helped back to things clean and fine. He thought of Euphemia, and just then his cousin spoke of her, eagerly, almost out of breath in her excitement:

"If we can only get Euphemia to go with us to-morrow. She always makes things move so smoothly, and looks out for everything, and you don't have to do a thing but have a good time. Everybody likes her, too, and you'll be crazy about her. Do you remember her? She's the youngest Martin girl.

The only thing is, everybody is after her. I don't know whether she can spare the time."

Lawrence Earle paused in the framing of an excuse for not going on the ride, and with sudden interest in the affair, and a new light in his eyes, said:

"Yes, by all means, Louise, get Euphemia to go!"

THE END

The publishers hope that this
Large Print Book has brought
you pleasurable reading.
Each title is designed to make
the text as easy to see as possible.
G.K. Hall Large Print Books
are available from your library and
your local bookstore. Or, you can
receive information by mail on
upcoming and current Large Print Books
and order directly from the publishers.
Just send your name and address to:

G.K. Hall & Co.
70 Lincoln Street
Boston, Mass. 02111

or call, toll-free:

1-800-343-2806

A note on the text
Large print edition designed by
Pauline L. Chin.
Composed in 16 pt Plantin
on a Xyvision 300/Linotron 202N
by Tara Casey
of G.K. Hall & Co.